Wesley "Joe" Davis
age 10, Moberly Lake, BC

Canadian Cataloguing Publication Data

Main entry title:
Just talking about ourselves

ISBN 0-919441-62-9 (v.1). --ISBN 0-919441-71-8 (v.2)

1. Canadian literature (English)--Indian authors. 2. Canadian literature (English)--20th century. 3. Indians of North America--British Columbia--Literary collections. 4. Youths' writings, Canadian (English) 5. Indian art--British Columbia. 6. Indian youth--Services for--British Columbia. I. Dolan, Marlena.
PS8235.16J87 1994   C810.8'09283   C94-910337-3
PR9194.5.15J87 1994

Credits:

The En'owkin Centre
Executive Director: Don Fiddler

Editor: Marlena Dolan

Editing Team:
    Candace Moon
    Barbara-Helen Hill

Health Canada, Medical Services Branch, Pacific Region
    Heather Walkus   Louise A. Wilson
    Robert Henderson   Patricia Wilson

Production and Design:
    Marlena Dolan

Dedication Page Design:
    Lynne Jorgesen, BC Hydro

Typesetting:
    Regina Gabriel
    Barbara-Helen Hill

Cover Art:
    Jim Logan, Kamloops, BC

The Publisher acknowledges the support of Medical Services Branch, Pacific Region of Health Canada, BC Hydro, The Canada Council and the Cultural Services Branch of the Province of British Columbia.

Printed in Canada.

"Just Talking About Ourselves"
Voices of Our Youth

Volume 2

Theytus Books Ltd.
Penticton, B.C., Canada

DEDICATION

Dreams are important to the spiritual, emotional, intellectual and physical well-being of all human beings. Without dreams, it would be almost impossible to visualize the better future we all desire for our descendants. B.C. Hydro is proud to participate in a project that encourages the creativity and vision of First Nations youth. We commend the strength and courage of the young people whose work appears on these pages, as their voices are a valuable contribution to greater understanding between all people.

BC hydro

Just Talking About Ourselves: Voices of Our Youth Volume 2

This publication is the second Anthology of a series of Youth Resource Manuals that is published for the Native youth of British Columbia. The poetry, short stories, personal essays and visual art tell their stories. This book is an invaluable tool in providing the youth with an opportunity to express themselves through their words and art. Many of the stories and poems inside these pages may break your heart, however, they are the realities and they must be heard.

As editor, I have selectively left error in some of the submissions. It is the intent of the book to best reflect the youth where they are in their lives, through their own words. The authors in this publication range from 10 to 21 years old; they all have a story and the right to tell it as they wish. Congratulations on their courage.

Without the generosity of Health Canada, Medical Services Branch, Pacific Region, and BC Hydo, this publication would not be possible. I thank them in their generosity in helping to provide the youth with this voice. I acknowledge the dedication of Heather Walkus and Rob Henderson in their continued support in this project.

As I read the submissions from the youth, I realize that we have a lot of very talented Native youth, whose courage and dreams are now forever recorded and shared. To them this volume is dedicated in the hope they they continue to dream and tell their stories.

Marlena Dolan
Editor

June, 1995

To Our Youth:

I'd like to share some thoughts about being young with you.

Youth is a very special time. It is a time of great change. Soon you will become young men and women.

Before the transition from youth to adulthood occurs allow yourself to experience what being young means.

There is a great excitement in being young. Most young minds are alert, ready to learn, inquisitive and adventurous.

Importance at this time of life revolves around matters such as fashion, music trends, hockey, football, baseball scores and generally enjoying time with your friends and family.

But being young can also be a time of great loneliness. It can be a trying time. Young people can feel unwanted, unloved or uncared for. Not all youngsters are as popular as others. Trying to fit in is not always easy.

The most important consideration at this time is your own worth, as it's easy to let your own worth go unrecognized.

Look deep inside and find a spark, nurse it and build on it. Soon your spark will shine. Protect it and nurture it and it will always provide the light you require on those dark lonely days.

The gifts we have as First Nations people are our families, our communities, our Elders and our culture. These things are what makes us proud people who thrive rather than merely survive.

In closing, I thank the Creator for each precious one of you.

Hai Hai, Thank you
Plains Cree Artist

George Littlechild

September 1995

Aboriginal Youth of British Columbia

It is my privilege to be able to speak to you upon the invitation of the Editors of this publication.

I grew up in a time when the pace was much slower than it is now. As a youth, I had the time to reflect and to get in touch with the community without being influenced by events or fads of many thousands of miles away. You do not have this luxury. You live in an exciting time and are the best informed youth of any age in history. Because of this, there are many choices you are faced with in life, and many influences outside the community. I want to tell you that it is a great time to be young and a great future is yours to enjoy. To help you realize the full measure of all of your expectations, I would like to suggest three things:

Don't be afraid to get in touch with your feelings. It is important to realize that the essence of spirituality is found at the feeling level of our being. At this level we learn to touch, to love, have empathy and to commit. Spirituality is feeling, not intellectualizing. It is letting the feelings we have inside, about the things we do guide us in the choices we have to make. In so doing, Creator will speak to us in new and powerful ways.

You are responsible for the choices that you make in life. No one can make you do what you do not choose to do, nor can you blame others for bad choices. The essence of sovereignty and autonomy is found in individuals who are not afraid to make tough choices and accept the responsibility.

Enjoy your life. You live in a time when there are many things to do and a time which can move too quickly, some times, for us to appreciate all the things that we have. Youth is a time to celebrate life in all its forms. Try not to move too fast nor travel too far, nor grow old too quickly. It is a precious time that those of us in our later years realize passes all too quickly.

Use this year to really get to know your family, your relatives, and your community. All the strength you need will be found there. My best wishes to you on your journey!

Don Fiddler
Executive Director, En'owkin Centre

September, 1995

To the First Nations Youth of British Columbia

I am honoured to write this letter for *"Just Talking About Ourselves" Volume 2*. I am grateful to the En'owkin Centre and their dedicated staff, Jeannette Armstrong, Marlena Dolan, Don Fiddler, Chick and their Board of Directors, who ensured the second publication of this very important book. Financial support from private and government organizations, corporations such as BC Hydro and the federal government's National Drug Strategy have also shown their commitment to ensuring the success of this publication.

The most important and critical gifts, however, are the thoughts and feelings of you, the First Nations youth of British Columbia. The honesty, integrity and openess in which you shared your lives, thoughts and feelings are really a testament to the power of your generation. This book and the ones to follow, is your history, your legacy to generations of youth unborn. This is important. If we know where we have been, we can better decide where we need to go and how to get there.

One of you asked me why this has just started—asking youth to publish their writing and art in their own way—without rigid themes, being graded, criticized, edited and grammar corrected. I have thought about that a lot. It seems to me that for several generations, in many communities, there were no, or very few, youth. They were at residential school. Also, many of your Grandparents spent years in Indian TB hospitals. Your generation is the first, legally allowed to live in your home community with your parents and family. Many of the usual rites of passage, learning and life skills were not passed on during that time. Our families and communities are still recovering from that. Your generation is making it possible to recover, with your ability to speak, write and draw your truths. This is a rare and new form of freedom that our people now have in what is called modern society. It was not too long ago that we were not allowed to vote, go to public school, raise and school our own children, teach our language and culture or leave and return to our communities, without seeking permission from the Indian Agent. These are truths of the generation before you.

In thinking about what I wanted to share with you, I read your stories and poetry and admired your art and I realized that there isn't much I could share that you haven't already thought about or know about. The one thing that did strike me though, was your hope and positive belief in your future. I really believe in that as well. If there is one thing I really want to share with you it is this; know that although in some areas the language and traditional practices are not wholly intact, the Creator is not dead. We did not lose everything. Those things we thought were gone, can come back through the truth that is your lives. What I think you have gained through the experiences of your Grandmothers and Grandfathers is never to accept someone else's view of who you are. You know down in your heart who you are and what you believe in and no other person, government agency, or system can take that away. Learn from the history and legacy of those generations before you so that you can ensure the safety and prosperity of the generations to come. This is the Indian way and will always be so . . . Thanks to you.

Halakasla
Heather Walkus, Health Planner, Upper Similkameen Indian Band

From the Past Into the Future — Joyce Joseph, age 17, Fountain (X'axlip) Band, Kamloops, BC

Indian Summer

As the sun gives warmth
and the animals give food
It's like how friends
give comfort
It's all in an Indian Summer.
An Indian Summer
comes and goes.
It's all part of life.

Tiger Isaac
age:12, grade: 7
Thompson Nlakapamuk

"Ancestoral Roots" Clint Donald, age 19, Sewepemc Nation, Kamloops, BC

.....Our

The Elders know of the years when the sun was hot.
When they watched as strangers came to the land.
The Elders know of the months when the sun was hot.
When they saw Mothers weep as uprooted youth dispersed like sand.

The Elders know of the years when the leaves fell.
Who watched as young men went in ships to war.
The Elders know of the months when the leaves fell.
Who saw families work hard for less, not more.

The Elders know of the years when the snow drifted.
And watched husbands take to axe and saw.
The Elders know of the months when the snow drifted.
And saw work in all weather until thaw.

The Elders know of the years when the rain dropped.
When they watched their people fight racism and tried to ignore it.
The Elders know of the months when the rain dropped.
When they saw them as one, with earth, sky and spirit.

Mark Matthew, age 15, grade 10
Shuswap Nation, Barriere, BC

Elders

Oh Great Grandfathers, please listen to my prayers:
I ask of you to look after my family and friends
I ask of you to make my spirit strong as bear's
I ask you to help us on what depends.
Oh Great Grandmothers, please do what you do in a good way:
By looking out for the creatures, winged, scaled, legged (two and four),
By making sure that what is taught is done in a good way each day,
By making our children further themselves by opening the door.
Oh Great Creator, please do what you have to do:
In doing so, let the people respect the land,
In doing so, let the ceremonies of our people live new,
In doing so, let our people proudly stand.
Oh Great Mother Earth, please hear my cries:
Our people depend on you and your gifts,
Our people still respect the animal that dies,
Our people look to you for spiritual lifts.
Oh Great Spirits, please look into my heart:
See that your help to our people is a must,
See that where we are today is just the start,
See that we need you to take pity upon us.
All my Relations

Roger Smith, age 17
Kamloops, BC

Our Elders

Before I begin my report I'd like to thank all the elders for their help. I'd like to begin with the land. First we have Thetis Island. There were posts of a Longhouse standing where Capenray Bible College is right now. We also learned that there is a grave yard over there somewhere too. We found that we owned Galiano Island; the area around Chemainus, Tent Island and a part of Salt Spring Island.

As for the Gun-boat, we heard several different stories. One of the stories was most often mentioned, and that was that the "Penelakut wouldn't sign a treaty with the Queen, that's why they tried to kill our people off."

We asked about Bone Game and found that women and children weren't allowed to play with men, we also learned that they used 21 sticks instead of 11. They used to bet blankets and shawls instead of money. Another thing is our people used to play on their knees instead of sitting on chairs.

When our elders would go out hunting they would be gone for days at a time. They would only come back when they had enough food to last for a while, meanwhile there would be some people out getting clams and some out picking berries, roots and teas. They would dry the berries and clams for winter. In case you ever wondered how our people used to cook without pots and pans, we were told that they would dig a big hole in the ground, line rocks inside it, make a fire and wait for the rocks to get hot. Then they took out the burnt wood and ashes and put about 6 to 10 sacks of clams onto the hot rock, after they sealed it with the sacks and some seaweed so the steam wouldn't escape.

It was almost the same with the way the meat was cooked except they had the meat wrapped in seaweed then wrapped in clay, while the rocks were being heated they had the meat sitting by the fire so the clay could get hard. When the rocks were ready they put the meat into the hole, the reason for the clay is because they wanted the meat to be cooked in its own juices.

I noticed back then, everyone had their share of chores, no one could just sit there and do nothing. It's obvious that our people knew how to be prepared for all seasons, and they knew how important it was to look after their family as well as themselves.

We asked elders what their most memorable moments were as children and most of them said spending time with their elders going out hunting, going for clams, and going berry or tea picking. Others said sitting after supper and listening to their elders tell all sorts of different stories.

Another thing we asked our elders is if they would like to say anything to our younger generation. Our results were that they would like to see every one getting along with one another instead of fighting, help parents with chores and food money, stop taking drugs and alcohol, and most important get an education. It's tough out there and it's going to get tougher if you don't have an education.

Joyce Johnny, age 19, grade 10
Penelakut Band, Chemainus, BC

As I . . .

As I walk down the street,
I see garbage on the ground,
drug deals going down on the corner
and innocent trees being hauled in to construct a new building.

As I watch the sunset,
I see smog fill the air,
I hear animals' hearts in sorrow as their species become extinct.
and I feel like the world is slowly ending.

As I dream at night,
I dream of our ancestors
walking into the rich forests for berries to pick,
wishing they were here,
to stop us from wasting our lives away . . .

Leah Joe
age:17, grade 12
Cowichan Tribe, Coast Salish Nation
Duncan, BC

Nikki Derickson
Okanagan Nation
Westbank, BC

Artwork - Donna Ermineskin

REMEMBERING

I sit on the sea wall
Watching the seagulls
Letting the time pass by

I sit in the mud and sludge
Watching the bullets fly by
And think, am I going to die?

I'm then back at the sea wall
The seagulls are gone
And time still passes
By

Men rush by me
As I lay in the mud
some, my friends,
Others I don't know

My friends are gone now
Just as the gulls
are
gone

But
Off in the distance
Just where the water meets the sky
I see another flock of gulls
Amongst the flock I see some wise ones

These ones are with us today
They are here to say
Stand up for what you believe in

Try not to fight
Negotiation is better than retribution
Love better than hate
Life better than fate

Robert (Bob) Wallas
Port Hardy, BC

One Man's Experience In The Army

My grandfather, as a young Native man, had dreams and expectations of what his life would be like. World War II changed those things but the changes were in himself and not in the world at home.

At the age of eighteen my grandfather left Kamloops to go to Vancouver on a freight train on December 14, 1941. When he left he had no job. His last job had been haying in the summer, and now he couldn't pay his rent and was leaving to Vancouver to find a job. He had one dollar in his pocket when he climbed onto a low bed freight car. He lost fifty cents while huddling between huge birch logs for several hours on the train. In his bag he had a camera and a few other personal belongings, this, and a dark green leather jacket were all he had to his name.

When he reached Vancouver he went to the unemployment office, he found a waiting line three people wide that extended around half a city block. After standing in this line for two hours and moving six feet he eventually gave up. He needed food so he pawned off everything he had for eight dollars. He ate at a Chinese restaurant.

Seeing limited options he decided to "join up" for the army. The next thing he knew he was in the back of a covered truck going to the recruiting office and from there to training camp in Vernon. He was trained as a gunner and went overseas. Due to impaired hearing caused by the excessive noise of gun fire, he ended up digging trenches. The 6 foot trenches that he and others dug were the same ones that his detachment slept in at night, usually while under fire.

After two years overseas, he had many experiences that changed him. He had been treated as an equal for the first time in his life. He seen death, lost friends and made friends both Native and non Native, but when he came back it was made quite obvious to him that nothing had changed at home. He was still an Indian, he was still an object of racism. He didn't have the right to vote and he didn't have the same privileges and freedom as the white soldiers who fought beside him overseas.

Mark Matthew
Age 15, grade 10
Shuswap Nation
Barriere, BC

Set Free

Although I'm scared to die
one day I must go
They'll take me way up high
To where I do not know
As my time will come
I'll hide all my fears
All the pain which I hold deep
Will flow through all my tears
I'll hold on so long
Until I'm blind to see
I'll soar through the sky
Alone I'm set free.

Carolyn Titley
age 17
Kamloops, BC

THE WORLD WAR II

My grandfather was in world War II. He went overseas to Europe. He was in the army. He went deaf from all the noise from the bombs and machines. My grandpa's name was Henry Seaweed. My grandfather was so nice to all his grandchildren. He always made all of us feel happy. He would give us money. I'd go see him every day and we'd all go to the mall to look around. My grandpa was 70 years old. He saw lots of his friends die. My grandpa was very sad because they were his best friends. My grandpa was happy to come home from the war.

> Casey Lancaster
> age: 14, grade 9
> Tlowitsis Mumtagila Band
> Port Hardy, BC

THE WINDS OF WAR

The winds of war they blow no more
over bloodstained battlefields

And the rivers that ran red from the masses of the dead
are refreshed by the passes of time

There are many who have died in waves of the sunset tide
furing the invasions from sea to shore

And the bodies they lay in the sand and the clay
as the surf laps against their lifeless remains

When the sun was high when the planes flew by
and brought devastation never seen before

The winds of war they blow no more
over bloodstained battlefieds

> Robert (Bob) Wallas
> Port Hardy, BC

Native Flag

The border and the design in the sun stands for that the Native people in Canada that they are good artists.
The bear stands for that there's a lot of wild animals in Canada.
The birds stands for that there's a lot of birds in Canada.
The fish stands for that some of the Natives in Canada eat.
White and black stand for eagle feathers.
Brown and red stand for the Natives.
Blue stands for fish and the sky.
Yellow stands for the sun and the south people.
The medicine wheel red stands for the east people, yellow stands for the south people, the black stands for the west people and the white stands for the north people.

Jody Charlie
Lytton First Nations
Lytton, BC

Jody Charlie, Lytton First Nations, Lytton, BC

The Picture

It was 2 o'clock in the morning, I couldn't sleep because of the nagging nightmare that's been haunting me for over a week. As I was trying to remember the details of the dream I heard a noise in my cellar. I leaped over to my closet and inside there lay the most dangerous weapon of all, a picture of my mother in law. I took the picture of her and being extra careful not to look at it, proceeded towards the cellar. As I was slowly inching my way towards the light switch near the bottom of my stairs, a very big, very strong, mean, vicious man was lumbering as fast as the speed of light in my direction. I could just see the features of this big ape. His biceps were as big as watermelons and his body as big as a blue whale. The veins in his forehead throbbing like they were ready to burst. Just in the nick of time I got to the switch, flicked it on as fast as I could and flashed the picture at this freight train of a man that was about to turn me into a welcome mat. The sounds of the feet pounding steadily into the concrete floor of the basement suddenly stopped, then following the silence of the darkness was a big thump. I looked and saw that it was my father lying on the floor half unconscious and frightened. When he came to he told me he was having a cigar because my mother wouldn't let him smoke, and he thought he heard a noise upstairs and was racing back trying to prevent himself from getting caught, he did not see me at the last second and almost slammed me against the wall, and fainted in terror because of the picture of my mother in-law.

Rick Alexis
age 16

Untitled

There was a time I thought I had died
They took a hold of me and didn't let go
I had never really tried,
I found it so hard to say no.

I had really hurt my dad
I myself thought I was cool
for some screwed up reason I didn't feel bad
My friends said I was a fool.

They made me feel so down
I finally thought I had them beat
I felt I was wearing a crown
When really they cut me like meat.

I would always ask to myself, ask
What is happening to me?
I felt I'm always wearing a mask,
I don't know who I want to be.

As I was going down hill
I felt like I was climbing a ladder
Somedays I felt like I could kill,
But did it really matter?

For some reason, I had a lot of fears
All I could see was the dying light.
I never thought I had any fears
I never thought the dark could get so bright.

I suddenly had no life in my eyes,
I kept on cursing my fate
Can't no-one hear my cries,
I will never get to heaven's gate.

Finally I reached that height
I finally rid all my pain
I finally pushed them out of sight,
Then really hard it started to rain.

Ed Redmond, Micmac Nation
age 19, grade 11
Kelowna, BC

Untitled

What is to be done for my next of kin to come? Will this chaos be here for them? Will they condemn my weakness or admire my spirit? Will I lighten and help to clarify this turmoil or will it increase from my efforts? Will I be here for them or them for me? My doubts shadow my future and my future shadows my presence here. Will they have my choices or will my choices make theirs disappear. If only my past was secured, perhaps it would secure theirs. And maybe I will endure this for a little longer, learn a little more before their time takes mine. Will my doubts be passed down or is it that a legacy will push them on and be their ground? As my ground is shaky because my sight is foggy. Will they remember my name? Will I remember the names which belong to me? My time is coming and it is already here. Please, let my eyes travel beyond this sphere. Perhaps their time will clarify mine. Then I will do all I can for my next of kin to come.

Joanna Recalma, age 16, grade 11
Kwakwaka'wak'w Nation, Qualicum Beach, BC

The Glass Wall

Sometimes I wish I could just talk to her.
But I wouldn't know what to say,
my thoughts are a blur.
It's like there's a glass wall blocking my way.
It keeps me from her everyday.
I can never touch her face or run my hands through her hair.
It hurts a lot because it is not fair.
Now I can't hear her and she can't hear me.
We can't be together, to speak of what might be.
Soon she begins to fade, she's getting harder to see.
I'm scared, confused, I want to flee.
I have the strengths to smash the wall to the ground.
This wall that robs me of touch, sight, smell and sound.
But in the past, all of the things that were said and done.
And to present, my will is next to none.
In the future, I hope our paths will cross once more.
And hope it will be different, not the same as before.
I take one final look at her, let out a deep sigh
Because I know for sure now it's "goodbye".

John Florence, age 19, grade 12
Katzie First Nation
Pitt Meadows, BC

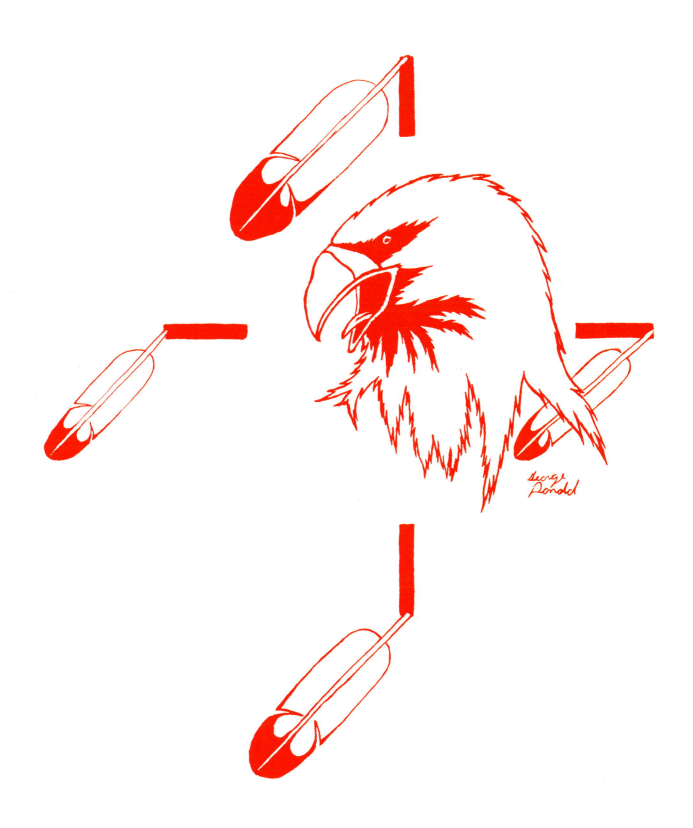

Four Directions - George Donald

Grandpa

*When I heard the news
pain gripped me. I lost control
and the anger took over. I fell to the floor
and I cried aloud
"No it can't be true"
As the hours have passed I
have not yet accepted it. I still hope
that maybe I will wake up
and sigh with relief "it was all a bad dream"
I know that this will never happen.
I know the truth,
but it has not yet been long enough to believe it.
As the time passes I will come to understand and
accept the answer to the question
that has been haunting my mind
since the beginning, "why?"
Until I am ready to accept the answer that will not happen.
I am feeling so much regret and pain
The regret is because there are
things that I wanted to say, and the
pain is caused by the fact that I lost you before I
said them. Grandpa why did
this all have to be so sudden?
Why did I not have the chance to say "Goodbye"
or tell you "I love you."
When people ask me what they can do to help
I want to say "find a way to bring him back for 2 minutes at least
or wake me up from this awful dream and allow me to tell him that
"I love him". I know that this is only a dream that will never happen
so I just say to them "nothing."
There is so much that I want you to be here for. There is so much
that I wanted you to see me
accomplish. Why did it have to be you?
Grandpa I know that you are only
physically gone because you are always
on my mind and you will always be in my heart.
I don't like the idea of going
on without you but I know what you would've wanted for me so that is why
I am going to fulfil my hopes and dreams.
Grandpa everything that I will accomplish will
be done for myself and you!
Grandpa I miss you and I love you!*

Melissa Michell, Lytton, BC

The Last Words of Death

Death is one last permanent vacation
remember, life's a journey not a destination
when the moment arrives nothing is alright
because with a blink of an eye, I'm gone tonight
just remember one thing, I'm with you all
and I know heaven's stairway is long and tall
I know all of you will now go insane
But hey! I'll help you walk through the guilt and pain
I know something will go wrong today
and I hope you all see things in a different way
My heart is with you all wherever you go
but whatever that is, take it easy and slow.

Lenore Hunlin
age 16, grade 11
Alexis Creek Band
Chilanko Forks, BC

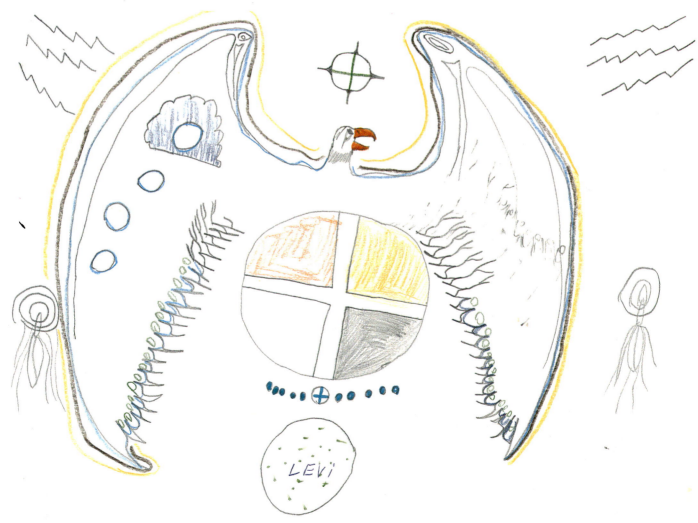

Artwork - Levi Parenteau

Friend . . .

When problems are there,
One way in & no way out . . .
Tears ready to fall,
But no where to land . . .

Nobody seems to care,
Silence becomes to shout . . .
Bad words being called,
No one to hold or to wipe your,
tears away . . .

But now you showed up,
I was ready to give up hope . . .
Lucky to have a friend like you,
I'll never need to be alone . . .

Korena "Koery" Peters
Cheslatta Carrier
Whut'en Nation
Burns Lake, BC

How it Feels

Do you know how it feels
When your mother is somewhere out there
Do you know how it feels
When your father is dead and gone
Do you know how it feels
When your only 16 years old

    Loss
    Pain
    Wonderment
    Suffering

Do you know how it feels
Growing up with strangers
Do you know how it feels
Having strangers call you son
Do you know how it feels
Calling strangers family

Do you know how it feels
To be adopted
Do you know how it feels
To have parents out of reach
Do you know how it feels
Probably not

    Confusion
    Torment
    Emotions
    Hurt

Do you know how it feels
Living a life not knowing your past
Looking for reconnection
Do you know how it feels
To be pushed around
Just for being different
Do you know how it feels
To be torn down
Teased all around
Do you know how it feels
To be loved by strangers
Who call you son

Do you know how it feels
With your mother somewhere out there
Do you know how it feels
To never be able to meet your father
Do you know how it feels
To be taken away from your own blood

Do you know how it feels
Having a million emotions run wild
Do you know how it feels
Knowing you were not wanted
Do you know how it feels
Being given up

Deep down it hurts
Deep down maybe it was a good thing
Deep down the pain lasts a lifetime
Deep down maybe you'd be better off dead

Do you know how it feels
To live an unchosen life
Do you know how it feels
Waiting for a brighter day
Do you know how it feels
To be taken from your family

Do you know how it feels
Not knowing the answer
Do you know how it feels
Being told lies
Do you know how it feels
To be adopted . . .

Bommer
Ojibwa Nation
age: 17, grade 11
Vancouver, BC

Boxing Day

I slothfully and limply inclined towards the window sill. I held my breath with what little strength I had left. If I exhaled, the water droplets of condensation would have disappeared forever, just like my hopes and dreams vanished yesterday and even within a matter of hours. Yesterday could have been the happiest day of my life but instead, some people that I counted on broke my heart into thousands of pieces, like a shattered window that was planned on being broken by an instigator. What I imagined to be a magical white Christmas, was a grotesque, ungratifying grey Christmas.

Today is Boxing Day. Today seems like a wonderful day, it looks new with a sparkling white blanket and the air is crisp and cool, now refreshing. My enraged anger is as high as the stars in the sky.

What a catastrophe. I despise Christmas. Since today is Boxing Day how about I box my whole life away. I don't ever want to see the colours red and green, to see little flashing lights, to ever hear those joyful Christmas carols, to ever smell a turkey not even on Thanksgiving Day, and to ever smell another evergreen tree again.

Maybe I will change my religion? (Never to celebrate Christmas again) All because of two irresponsible alcoholics, my parents. The joy of Christmas was gone away, gone away like a runaway. For me, December 25th is just another day.

I am now 16. In about a year and a half I will complete grade 12. I have a grade point average of 4.0 and how proud my foster parents are of me. They say that I am a rare person of my type. I never understood.

I was adopted at the age of not even 48 hours. My so-called mother was only 16 when she gave birth to me, now she is 32 and my father . . . . .

I've always wondered why the colour of my skin was darker than everyone else around me. It seems like I was always the only darker one but I never thought anything of it. Last year, on my 15th birthday I finally asked. Gail, my foster mother, explained everything to me as well as she could but it dramatically changed my life. Yesterday, it only took a few hours to shatter everything.

Ever since I knew the truth, I wanted to find my real parents. I wanted to know everything. I wanted to know who I was. The only Christmas present I wanted was to go home with my parents and let them be proud. I never really thought of questions like why did my mother give me up?

Why didn't they ever come looking for me? Don't they care? Not until, the day they never showed up.

I was patiently, but very eagerly waiting upon their arrival. The tree was full of vibrant, exhilarating, flashing, bright colours, candy canes on every other branch, tinsel shining in the room, ornaments of extraordinary meaning and the star at the top was the finishing touch. Christmas music was gently playing in the background, the aroma of the freshly cut evergreen filled the air and the smell of Christmas dinner close by.

I waited and waited and waited for the doorbell to ring or the phone for an explanation. Every noise I jumped. There was a stillness and quietness that lingered in the room, for my heart was not there. The anguish, the pain that I felt. Tears fell as I waited for someone to walk up the steps, someone that resembled me. I swear, as much as I cry, I can create my own lake. My eyes resembled those of the neighbourhood druggie. I didn't know what to think or how to feel? I am only 16 and trying to discover who I am. I am so confused . My mind is boggled with questions and more questions. But of course they are unanswered.

Today, all I know is that my parents are Gail and Jeremiah C. and therefore the people who conceived me are 2 Native Indians that are alcoholics and are missing out on a wonderful person. Reality hit me, they aren't going to come, they're too busy drinking their life away. Obviously, they drove me away. I'll never forgive. NOTHING at all can cure the pain that is in my heart.

I am boxing my life away. Not just the Christmas stuff but a lot more. I wish I never relied on their arrival. I despise Christmas which is supposedly, the most joyous holiday. I do not know who I am.

Leateequia A. Daniels
age: 16 grade: 11
Saanich, BC

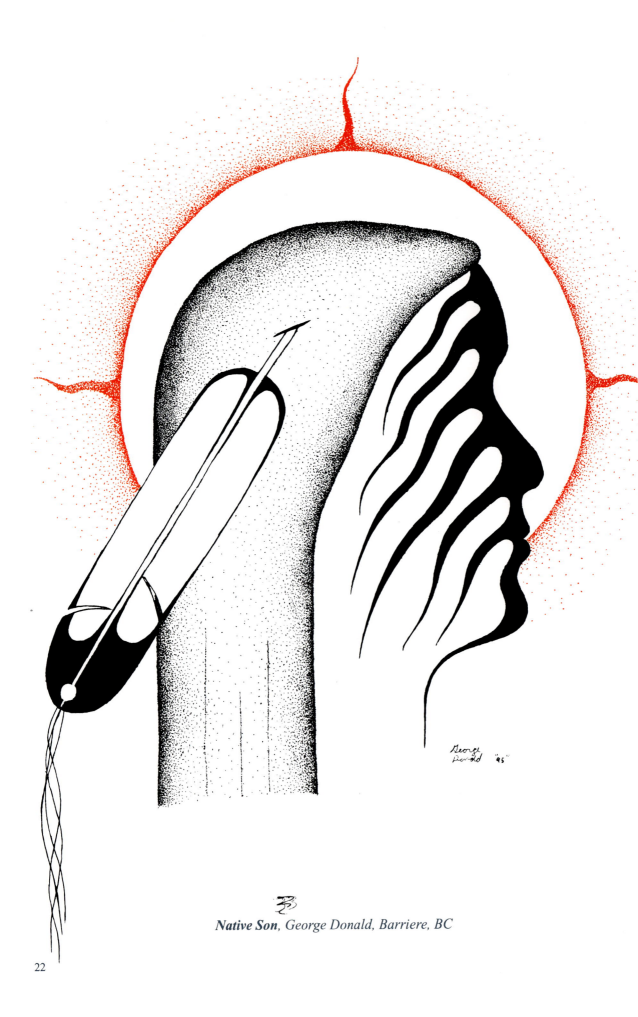

Native Son, George Donald, Barriere, BC

Olivia's Lesson

The punch knocked Olivia to the ground. She struggled to regain consciousness, as blood flowed off her chin from her broken lip. Jack laughed as he swaggered in front of her. He had short, blonde hair, almost like a brush cut, and he wore blue, faded, torn Levi's with a black leather belt. He also had black steel-toed boots, a white Suicidal Tendencies t-shirt and a gun in his back pocket.

"If you even dare to go near my sister again, I'll torture you to death." Jack yelled as he clenched his fists and kicked her in the stomach.

Olivia curled into a ball, holding her stomach. Jack kicked her again, this time on the back. "You stupid worthless welfare drunken Indian" he said through his teeth. He spit on her, then she heard him walk away. She looked and saw him giving his friend a high-five as they climbed into their old white corvette.

She felt like she could hardly breathe and she was in too much pain to cry. Pushing herself up with one hand and holding her stomach with the other, she sat up. Her legs were sore and bruised badly from being kicked. The cut on her lip and the scrapes on her arms stung. Her cheeks hurt badly and she could barely open her right eye.

Moving her hair out of her face, Olivia looked around. She wasn't far from home because she could see the reserve houses about one quarter of a mile down the road, through the trees. She was sitting on the side of the gravel road, and rows of tall pine trees were lined up along each side of the dirt road. The sun was setting behind the mountain and the only sounds were of trees rustling from the wind and a train in he distance.

Olivia slowly stood up, cringing from the pain, and took a few steps. Her legs hurt badly. Olivia slowly made her way home trying her hardest to keep from falling.

At the reserve, Benny, who just happened to look out the window, saw Olivia staggering home. Her long dark hair was messy and her jeans and t-shirt were rugged and dirty. She looked like she had trouble keeping her balance, and Benny knew that Olivia never drank, and even if she did it would be with him.

Within seconds Benny was out the door and calling to Olivia. "Olivia, hey, are you all right?" he asked. Olivia turned around shocking Benny by what he saw. She had a black eye which was puffed up and swollen and she had a big cut on her bottom lip. Her left cheek had a big dark purple and black bruise, her arms were all scraped up, and the blood was drying up into scabs. She also had blood stains on her clothes.

"Whoa, woman, what the hell happened? You get into a fight?" Benny asked in shock. Olivia couldn't answer. A lump was welling up inside her throat and she started to cry. "Come on, you got to get cleaned up." Benny said as he gave her a hug and tried to comfort her.

He led her inside her house were nobody was home, but the TV. had been left on.

"I'll get myself cleaned up, you can wait here." Olivia said as she wiped the tears from her face. He wanted to help her but he stayed put, and sat on the couch in front of the television set and waited.

Olivia was Benny's best friend. They had known each other all their lives. He felt so sorry for her, being beaten up like that. "Damn, poor Olivia, why did she have to get hurt, why her?" he asked himself in his mind. He had a feeling he knew exactly what happened. He knew that she had an enemy in school named Josie, who was white, conceited and blond. Her hair was cut neatly short too, and she was the same age as them, seventeen. She always wore black combat boots, tight blue jeans and white t-shirts tucked in her jeans.

Josie's not that tough. She couldn't hurt Olivia like that but she would get her brother after her. He was slow enough to do that. They are the kind of people who believe that white people are superior over all the other races. They think they should be privileged.

As Olivia walked into the living room she saw Benny sitting on the couch in front of the TV. He was staring at it but she could tell that his mind was elsewhere. He had a Georgetown cap on and had long, dark hair like her own. He wore a black turtleneck underneath a white t-shirt, and baggy blue jeans on.

Looking up, Benny asked what actually happened. "Well, it basically started up yesterday when I was getting pissed off at Josie. She tried to act tough by bullying me around, trying to push me around, then I just punched her and told her to f --- off. I'm the one who got in trouble too, because she told on me, and the witnesses were on her side. The teachers just phoned my mom, but I didn't get suspended. Anyway she told her . . . "

"Wait, why did she just start pushing you around for anyway?" Benny asked, interrupting her.

"She was giving a bunch of wrong facts about Natives and I was getting mad. She should have just stated her opinions instead of lying like that. We were just arguing or debating then she started to put me down personally. She goes, "You're a loser, quitter, and you're an idiot." Then she started acting tough" Olivia told him.

"Okay, then she probably told Jack right?" he asked.

"Yeah, after I decked her she started screaming at me and threatening that her brother will come after me. I just said "Go away you piece of conceited white trash, and she looked like she wanted to kill me. I should have just laughed" Olivia said. "I bet that would be the last straw if you did." Benny said.

"Well anyway, today I had to walk home from school by myself and I was kind of scared because you stayed home . I kept hoping that every car I saw and heard would go right by, and leave me alone because my grandma always talks to us about walking home alone and that anyone could pick us up and take us away". Benny nodded in understanding. "I heard a car behind me and I kept thinking "go right by please go right by," and then I thought I heard it pull over so I turned around to look and I saw Jack's white '77 Camero pull over and I really freaked out. I started to run but I couldn't get my legs to move very fast. Then I think it was Jack who caught me by my hair and I fell backwards on the ground and then they beat me up." Olivia explained.

"Geez, I think that's pretty shallow of Jack. Having two other guys to back him up while they stock you down when your by yourself." Benny stated.

"Well I'm going to be visiting my grandma as soon as my mom gets home anyway. My sister is staying at my aunts house so me and my mom will be going when she gets home." she told him.

Olivia loved visiting her grandmother. She had a small grey house which was always warm, but not too hot and stuffy. The house was always tidy and the couches had crocheted afghans draped over them. She had pictures of her family all over the walls and had a cedar shelf filled with stone carvings mostly made by one of Olivia's uncles. The house smelled sweet from the cakes she usually baked.

While Olivia told her grandmother everything that had happened in their Native language, her grandmother made her some herbal medicines. She made some for her scrapes, cuts and bruises and she made some hot liquid that is kind of like tea.

After that her mom and her grandmother started talking about their values. Then her grandma started telling lots and lots of stories about incidents of racism, fighting, and strange beliefs of some people. Her grandmother also taught her some songs that help you feel better. Those songs are what she learned from her grandmother.

The next morning Olivia woke up feeling much better. Through the stories she had learned a lot, and with the song she had learned she gained something special. She sang the song in her mind over and over. She felt like she could deal with her problems now.

In school Josie ignored Olivia. Her and her friends looked at her and laughed, but Olivia didn't pay any attention. It didn't bother her. They can think what they want and believe what they want. She couldn't control them. She didn't have to talk to Josie again.

Alissia Lytton
age 16, grade 11
Nicomen Band
Lytton, BC

Words of Wisdom

In our changing world, we see many problems ranging from drug/alcohol addiction to environmental problems. Many people feel it is too late to "clean up" our acts. But it isn't.

The last thing we need is grade 8 students drug dealing in schools and nine year olds smoking. What's worse is there aren't any role models to stop them and teach them the right way of life. The parents may be too involved in their work, or too stoned or drunk themselves. If the children are taught what's right for them, they'll teach their children and soon the world would be a cleaner place.

The rainforest is a hot issue being discussed and dealt with. But more getting involved and taking action would contribute to a healthy rainforest. Trees are getting wiped out. There's just no end to it if the problems don't get slowly resolved. The trees should be used for the nature's cycle, not the furniture cycle.

Long ago, our ancestors would go into the forest for medicine taken from the plants. Food was found in the wild and shelter was the whole forest. Today, doctors replaced the medicine man, stores replaced the forest. Every day 5 sq. kilometres are wiped out for one fast food outlet.

A mall carrying 48 stores wiped out one reserve. If we stand and list our rights for saving our world from these "dirty deeds", our grandchildren would be happier and they will know who to thank.

Leah Joe, age 17, grade12
Coast Salish Nation, Duncan, BC

Baby I love your way . . .

I know I didn't say yes,
When you ask me to be your girlfriend . . .

Please let you guess,
sure . . . but I'll never want to end being friends . . .

When you ask me to owl dance,
I said "no" then you charged me . . .

Baby I love you,
BUT this is more than I can handle . . .

Sure I want to be with you,
NOT now, but later, when you know what you want . . .

So you say . . . okay friends it is then,
I'll say "Baby I love your way"

Korena Peters - Cheslatta Carrier
Whut'en nation, Burns Lake, BC

Fetal Alcohol Syndrome

*A*re you willing to jeopardize your unborn babies life by drinking alcohol during pregnancy? Fetal Alcohol Syndrome [F.A.S.] is a relatively new field of study. It affects not only the growth and performance of the child, but also results in head, facial and limb abnormalities, as well as the defects of the heart. Because Fetal Alcohol Syndrome is a new problem with such devastating results, we need to look at the symptoms, the cause and the prevention of this syndrome.

The symptoms of this syndrome can be very hard for parents and children to cope with. It is not unusual for babies to be born with alcohol on their breath when the mother has gone through labour intoxicated.

> It wouldn't be so bad if it (F.A.S.) just resulted in smaller brain size, but it affects the brain, destroying brain cells resulting in smaller brain size and mental deficiency. The brain never catches up afterward. (Pawlak - Frazier)

The rate of linear growth is about two thirds that of the norm. Children who have fetal alcohol syndrome tend to gain weight more slowly and are described as "failing to thrive" in which they must be hospitalized. Some of the lucky children, as they approach adolescence, develop better weight to height ratio and no longer give the appearance of being undernourished or ill. Also many with heart defects heal spontaneously but others require open heart surgery to correct this problem. However the brain is not so forgiving for the I.Q. doesn't seem to improve with age. The child with F.A.S. becomes mentally and socially backwards. Many F.A.S. children as high as 43%, become the wards of the state because of the mother's continued alcoholism. Even with the best foster care and early infant stimulation programs, the children remain in many ways handicapped. Once we have recognized the symptoms of this syndrome, we must look carefully at what caused these abnormalities.

The cause of this syndrome is actually quite simple because it involves alcohol. Much remains to be discovered regarding the origin and progression of F.A.S. It is certain that alcohol crosses the placenta barrier in approximately the same concentration as in the mother. It is theorized the forming child is ill equipped to handle and metabolize the alcohol. Since the babies organs aren't fully operational yet, the result is the destruction of cell tissue within the fetus. Because the original cell tissue develops into other cells, then all of the baby's cells would be damaged as well. All of the future cells would develop from them. In this theory, the direct toxicity of the alcohol itself, or an intermediate metabolite, is likely the destructive agents. Researchers have suggested that it is the malnutrition that accompanies alcoholism which is the real demon. Over 80% of F.A.S. children have a fine motor dysfunction, development delay and/or mental deficiency. 97% have pre and post natal deficiency. Usually children of F.A.S. have small heads, short eye slits and defective development of mid-facial tissue. Also they have inner epicanthel folds and minor outer ear abnormalities. Some of these children have abnormal creases in the palm of their hand and minor abnormalities of the joints. About 50% of these children have a heart defect in the wall separating the chambers. A few of these children have slight genital defects and a benign tumour of the blood vessels in infancy. Because we know alcohol is a factor, we should prevent women from drinking during pregnancy.

> Prevention is the only way we could help stop this syndrome from occurring so frequently. One of the steps towards prevention of F.A.S. is education of the public as to the risk of alcohol use during the gestation period. (Pawlak-Frazier)

In this manner it is hoped that every chronically alcoholic woman can be made aware of the possible consequences. Birth control should be used as long as a woman remains an alcoholic or as an alternative, abortion may be made available. The best prevention is to stop drinking; because a "SAFE" alcohol level has not yet been established. From both the findings in human and animal studies, there is no risk of F.A.S. if the alcohol has been discontinued before and during pregnancy. The life and health of an unborn is delicate and, remember, F.A.S. is preventable. Unless we prevent pregnant women from drinking alcohol, we will have many more F.A.S. children.

Any woman who even suspects she's pregnant shouldn't drink alcohol because of the risk of having a child with Fetal Alcohol Syndrome. Such a child would be condemned to a life of limited ability. The other family members would suffer as well because the child with F.A.S. would get most of the attention and the other children would think they were getting left out. Also caring for that child would probably be very expensive because of the problems the child would have like heart problems, special teachers for school, and expensive medical equipment. So all those pregnant mothers out there should stop and think before they take a drink.

Works Cited
Pawlak - Frazier, Pamela and Daniel. <u>Fetal Alcohol Syndrome</u> n.d.

Sheila Williams, age 15, grade 10
Tsawwassen First Nation
Coast Salish, Delta, BC

The Miracle in The Forest

Once in an enchanted forest there lived a woman named Diane. She was beautiful, more beautiful then any other princess in any other town. Diane had long blond hair, and sparkling blue green eyes. Diane's figure was just perfect, and her voice was as beautiful as she was. She sounded like a dove.

However even with all her beauty she could not get any money from anyone. Diane was poor. But she could always find food to eat because of the enchanted forest. It always had coconuts, bananas, cherries and blueberries. So she had no problem with food what so ever.

One day Diane was walking in the forest, suddenly she heard a cry. Diane wondered what was making that noise, so she went looking for it. After looking for hours she had finally found it. For it was a little baby. Diane watched him constantly.

When the baby got older Diane named him Kyle. She had always wanted a baby named Kyle. Over the years Kyle grew more and more apart from Diane. One day Kyle was selected king. It was then he realised that he really needed his mother. (He thought of Diane as his mother). So he went to pick Diane up unexpectedly, but when he got there his mother (Diane) did not recognize him. When she realised it was Kyle, she fell into shock. Suddenly he picked her up and he carried her to his carriage.

When he got into town, he bought his mother the most expensive clothing money could buy. And the most expensive jewellery money could buy.

With her money and everything it solved two of her problems. One was to have more clothing and the other was to have more money. The lesson of this story is to remember the people who brought you up.

Dorothy Andrew, age 12
Homalco Band
Campbell River, BC

Skate Boarding
fast   hard
ball   talent   smoothness
landing   tricks
sponsored

Soccer
aggressive   fun
pass   score   kick
sport of the world
football

Skate contest
He neared the stairs fast
and knew all eyes watched him now
kick, flip, rolls away.

Kyle Scow, age 15
Kwakiutl Band
Port Hardy, BC

Artwork Cassie Adams
Grade 8, 13 years old
Lytton First Nation

Aboriginal Rights

What do Indian [First Nations] people want? (Riley 159) The main thing that First Nations people want is basic human rights. They have been taken away from First Nations, and it's time to get them back. The original contracts and treaties that First Nations signed with the Europeans failed to represent the needs of the First Nations people fairly. More changes need to be made and research is needed on treaties, cultural rights, and land claims.

Therefore Aboriginal rights are "ownership of land and resources, cultural rights, legal recognition of tribal laws, and the right to self-government." (Henderson 2). These will give First Nations people independence and dignity, but these are difficult to gain. To achieve all of the above, Natives need the negotiation process improved, the courts need to be more enthused to deal with issues about the basic human rights for Natives, and more enforcement of constitutional acts is needed.

The treaties signed by the Europeans and First Nations people took unfair advantage of the First Nations people. Europeans showed absolutely no respect for the Native culture what so ever, and there was also a language barrier the Europeans didn't want to climb over. To this day "there are no treaties for the Natives of British Columbia" (Riley 156) but many Native lawyers are working on the process of treaty agreements which is a long and tiring process.

The land claims have been a topic of debate for several years now, since they were designated in an unfair manner too! For example, the Tsawwassen Coast Salish people only have 20-30 acres of housing land for 300 people on the reserve.

Native land claims is an enormous and complex topic; there are many Native communities which do not have enough land even for a quarter of an acre per person. The treaties need to be rewritten in a fair manner; cultural rights need to be looked at by the government and the court systems. Once new laws are in place, the government, the courts and all police departments must recognize them and enforce them. Then there are also land claims which still need to be negotiated, evaluated, restructured and designated by the government.

Joe Williams, grade 10
Tsawwassen First Nation
Coast Salish

DARK

Dark has many meanings
Death, hate, emptiness.
Dark is by my side next to
light — holding hands but hating
each other. No way to break them
apart. To me there is more Dark
than light

Andrew Loring
Age 16, grade 12
Lytton First Nations

Wish We All Could Be Free!

I, as a person, have a right to live freely
just like whales and eagles live freely
Out in the open, nice, quiet, blue ocean
able to swim freely and enjoy the breeze
that is blown among their faces, jumping
and splashing one another, playing together.
soon will be mating, having soon brought
life into the world and will hopefully
continue is what I'm thinking
The eagle to be flying up there ever so
freely, looking for food, in the waters; the
waters that the whales are swimming
Later, off to the nest to bring the younglings
food, crying as their mother comes into sight
We all should be able to walk out in the public
without any fear of someone jumping out at
them. I as the eagle crying out for help not for
food but for love, comfort and support. I, like
the whale, am able to walk freely and not
having to worry, because I live in a better
environment than others.

Bernadette Claire, age 16
Quatsino Band
Coal Harbour, BC

Suicide

In Canada we have one of the highest standards of living. Why, in a desirable a country like ours, do we have such a high number of teenage suicides? More than 100,000 young people between the ages of ten and twenty-four attempt suicide every year.

The suicide rate among teenagers has tripled since 1950 (Karlsberg 28). To prevent young people from committing suicide as an end to their pain without thinking of the hurt they cause to others, community support and education must be provided for distressed youth.

Teenage suicide is a serious problem in our society for many reasons. One is that teenagers have been known to have low self-esteem because of child abuse when they were younger. Also it could have been the parents' fault because of divorce, family break-ups or unemployment.

"Dr. Richard Seiden, has suggested that alcoholism, unemployment, cutbacks in social services, and academic competition contribute to many suicides that occur among youths between the ages fifteen and twenty-four by encouraging widespread depression and loss of self-esteem. Add to those pressures, such sad facts of life as divorce, family break-up, and the fear of nuclear war." (Langone 53) Child abuse is also another social problem that can contribute to youth suicides. Also their social conditions may be blamed for suicides.

According to Dr. Paul Safran, Ph.D., "Many teens believe that if they try to commit suicide, and kill themselves, they'll come back again to see how people react to their death." He also says, "they may even fantasize about their death." He also says, "they may even fantasize about their funeral. They do not realize the finality of [the act]. Their thinking just does not allow them to. They think they're immortal that nothing will happen to them." (Karlsberg 29) The teenagers don't even consider how their family, friends and relatives will react to the teen's death. The teenagers are not aware of the copy cat effect which may cause others to contemplate suicide too. Teenagers don't realize that their death will make their friends and family very upset, sad, and lonely. Teenagers should not commit suicide because there's so much they will miss in life: their problems can be solved and suicide can be prevented. Teens are very selfish when it comes to suicide: they don't consider how their death will affect other people.

Society needs to provide support, education, counselling and activities to prevent our young people from committing suicide. Communicating their problems to others could help teenagers take suicide off their minds and that will also make them think that you really care for them. Suicidal teens can talk to anyone, their friends, counsellors, parents or even teachers, but before they tell anyone, they should consider carefully, whom they tell, and choose a person they know will listen to them and understand. Another way to help prevent suicide would be, "Get the attention of someone who cares, a kindred spirit, that can help restore their will to live and give the suicidal person enough strength to survive the crisis, to hang on to the alternate, until a more solid solution can be found" (Langone 110).

Communication, support and education must be provided to prevent people from committing suicide. Volunteers have recognized that a suicide attempt is almost always "a cry for help" (Langone 110).

Natasha Williams, grade 10
Delta, BC

Works Cited

Karlsberg, Elizabeth. "Teenage Suicide." Teen. April 1992:
    24,25,28-29

Langone, John. Dead End. Canada: Little, Brown, 1986

No One Knows

No one knows
how I feel inside
No one knows
but me
No one knows
I feel trapped inside steel bars
and can't get out
I don't want anyone to know
I feel hurt, tired, and scared
While on the outside
I try to cover it with
laughter and smiles
No one knows
Everyday
I seem to grow more scared
of life
Still, No one knows why
Not even I
Maybe later on in life
I'll find out why

Charlene Young, age 14, grade 9
Haida Nation
Massett, Queen Charlotte Islands

Fade to Black

The emotions not spoken are the ones that hurt the most, to know the feelings are strong, will disappear because of my weakness. When I keep the really deep down feelings to myself, I feel that it is suffocating me and the pressure is coming to me, all at the same time when I am broken down. As I see sadness in those eyes of my cherished ones. It just tears me apart, because I want to search deep down for the write words, that will make sense. I just want to do something for they're broken down emotions. The words you can't communicate to others are also the words from your heart are the most that are unspoken. What comforts me is the friendship and the in common things also joking and laughing. I am afraid of letting too much out because the power another person could have over your weakness.

Kelly Alphonse
Williams Lake, BC

The Time When I Was Scared

The time I was most scared was when I was about 13 years old. I was with my uncle riding around in his new car. He was drunk and he was swerving all over the road. I told him to slow down but he wouldn't listen; he just went faster and faster. About ten minutes later, we drove past my grandmother's house. He went off the road, just missed a ditch, went into a driveway, and hit a cement post. The car flipped in the air about three times and landed in some body's yard. My uncle went through the windshield and flew about ten feet away from the car. But lucky for me I was buckled up. I just got a broken arm from all of that trouble. It didn't take long for the cops and the ambulance to get there. They had trouble getting me out of the car because I was jammed in. It took about fifteen minutes to get me out of the car. I got in trouble with my parents because I wasn't supposed to be out with him.

Bert Jefferson
Tsawwassen First Nations
Delta, BC

I AM AFRAID

I am afraid of you drinking

I am afraid of you fighting

I am afraid of you hitting
each other

I am afraid of you being sick
when you are drunk

I am afraid of you running away
when you are drunk

I am afraid of you not being there
for me when I need your help.

What will I do if I really need your
help

Where are you going to be when I
need your love and support.

Shannon Spinks, grade 7, age 11
Lytton First Nations
Lytton, BC

Deadly Party

You went to a party,
you had a drink.
You knew it was wrong,
Didn't you think?
You partied all night,
You smoked a joint.
Were you acting cool?
What was your point?
These things are
dangerous,
Don't you care?
Or do you
Actually think,
You have a life to spare?

Chrissy Sam
Lytton, BC

Artwork - Justin Terbasket
Okanagan Nation
Keremeos, BC

The Negative Effects of Alcohol

Alcoholism runs in the families. Study after study has shown:

> the majority of all alcoholics come from families in which one or more members-parent, grandparent, sibling, even aunt or uncle — have had a drinking problem. Studies also show that children of alcoholics are at an especially high risk of developing drinking problems. (Ryerson 21)

Going out to parties with one's friends may seem like a lot of fun, but being addicted to alcohol condemns a person to a life of all illness, poverty, loneliness, abuses and violence. Adults who drink to excess bring on themselves health problems, behaviour problems and worst of all, family problems.

An alcoholic develops many health problems because of his drinking. Most alcoholics would rather drink than eat. As a result, they have "malnutrition and vitamin deficiency. Lack of vitamins makes them prone to infections and upper respiratory ailments. Excessive alcohol intake affects the respiratory ailments. Excessive alcohol intake affects the production and activity of certain disease — fighting white blood cells, giving the alcoholic particularly low resistance to bacteria." Eventually an alcoholic may develop the chirrohis of the liver which will eventually kill him. Stomach and gastrointestinal ailments, heart disease, kidney failure. Other problems alcoholics have are ulcers, gastritis, inflammation of the pancreas, and cancer of the stomach. Very heavy drinkers have lowered resistance to pneumonia and other infectious disease.

The behaviour of an alcoholic is influenced by his use of alcohol. Some alcoholics go to work or school intoxicated which often results; in their being fired. Alcohol affects a person's driving skills; he is lucky if he does not kill himself or others while drinking impaired. Anyone who goes to work intoxicated endangers himself and his fellow workers. Often, while impaired, an alcoholic will do something that "he contends he would never do without alcohol"(Lee 89). He goes on frequent drinking sprees which result in blackout and passouts.

The family of the alcoholic also suffer from his drinking. One child of an alcoholic expressed his suffering this way:

> How could I take it as a slight to me that someone else was praised? It shows how truly needy I was of getting support and attention — again because I was getting none of those at home. I can explode at the slightest thing, adds Timothy. I never knew what was going to set me off. If any of my friends mention drinking or parents, it's like a switch goes off and I want to lash out at him. Sometimes I want to jump up and hit him. It's weird. I get over critical of people a lot of times. (Ryerson 27)

Children of the alcoholics are neglected; in fact they often have to look after their parents. This is because the parents don't keep promises to their own children. That's why they only spend their money on beer, so they drink too much alcohol and they don't have enough to buy food, clothes and the kids needs. When they drink, they get into a big argument about small issues and larger ones. Sometimes these arguments become violent and the parents start fighting in front of the kids.

> An alcoholic's health behaviour and family are all negatively affected by his drinking. Experts are so concerned about the number of young people who are

using alcohol today. Says one psychiatrist, "they are, in effect, getting a head start on the disease. The junior high student who drinks occasionally may not be dependent on alcohol today. Nevertheless, he or she is building up a tolerance to the substance and, by the time he reaches the age of twenty-five or thirty, may have a full blown alcohol problem" (Englebardt 33,34).

Alcoholism is a deadly disease which teenager can prevent by not drinking alcohol. Teenagers who live with alcoholics need help which they can seek through Al-a-teen, psychiatrist, school counsellor, a trust worthy friend or teacher.

Terri Splockton
Tswawwassen First Nation
Delta, BC

Works Cited
Englebardt, Stanley L. <u>Kids and Alcohol, The Deadliest Drug.</u>
New York: Lothrop Lee and Shepard, 1975

Lee, Essie. <u>Alcohol - Proof of What?</u>
New York: Julian Messner 1976

Ryerson, Eric. <u>When Your Parents Drink Too Much.</u>
New York, 1985

Is This the Way You Want To Say Goodbye?

Here we are at wonderful Port Hardy. With teenagers full of energy and excitement. On Fridays there are parties at a place called "Lagoon Lake", I guess you could say it has it's strange moments.

I remember coming from there a few times right out of it, the same as I was this particular evening. I was carried out of the party to a car. I was so tanked that I didn't even realize the car I was in was being driven by someone as intoxicated as myself. The car ended up in a six foot ditch. I don't remember being taken out of the car, I didn't even acknowledge the fact that I had been in an accident.

The only good thing I did that night was before I started drinking I had made arrangements with my girlfriend to look after me while I partied. Many of my friends and I have this agreement because being girls under the influence seems to draw the boys who think they can take advantage of a drunk girl.

After the accident I was walking around with my friend who was looking after me, she couldn't understand what I was saying. My head was spinning with thoughts and questions. I wonder now if it was the alcohol and the accident combined. But my thoughts were blurring, spinning in my head — what am I doing here?, where am I?, and who am I with? I wanted to go home but the only ride available was going only half way to town. I was confused, wandering around now by myself, shaking my head. My friend approached me asking what was wrong, not wanting to attract attention I said "nothing".

We found our ride home and when we got in I just wanted to pass out and drift away from the world around me and from the people with me. I did exactly that. Except I drifted too far away. My heart stopped. I could feel myself slipping away slowly. Everything was faded and a blur. I wasn't sure of what was going on but I knew that what ever was happening felt good. I was at peace and didn't want to go anywhere else. I thought so little about what I was leaving behind. All I could see was my family standing there watching me float into the bright light. They were waving good bye to me and I waved back. It was like I didn't want to go but I wouldn't fight to stay and they wouldn't fight for me to stay. It was like they knew and understood why I was leaving. They knew that I was at peace and that I was happy right where I was.

Now I know what it would be like to die. It was very peaceful, but that's not the way I wanted to go. Nobody wants to go like that. I was intoxicated. But I was given a second chance and I was lucky. I learned my lesson and I learned it the hard way.

There's a lesson to be learned here for all. If your going to drink just make sure you are with someone that will keep an eye on you. Judgements made by intoxicated people could be life threatening, such as climbing into a car driven by another intoxicated person. If someone is watching out for you then they can help direct you when you are walking in your dream induced alcohol state.

This story was taken from real actual events of teenagers and put together in story form.

Janet Hanuse, age 17
Gwa'sala-'Nakwaxda'xa Band
Port Hardy, BC

Mom

*Mothers are the best you can get,
They allow you to get their shoulder wet
I am so blind that I cannot see,
How much my mother loves me.*

*We've been through good and bad,
We've made each other sad
When I left I didn't know
How much I'd miss her so.*

*I was so sad I couldn't see,
But now I want her to be a part of me.
I saw her picture last night
And I remembered our last fight
I held so many things inside,
so many times I've sat and cried*

*I want her to know
I love her so
I'll always be here,
so close; so near.*

*Never have I told her a lie,
But it hurt so much to see her cry,
I know what she told me about life is true,
But understand, I live in a dream-world,
not reality like you.
I want life to be perfect in every way,
I know perfectness just goes away.
I'm writing this for you, from me,
my heart and feelings too.
I just want to say, Mom, I love you.*

*Aimee Lezard, age 17
Okanagan Nation
Penticton, BC*

HOW MY MOM CHANGED HER LIFE

My mom started drinking with all her friends. After that we told my mom that we didn't want her to drink. She said she was having too much fun with her friends. She always left me and my brother with a mean baby-sitter. One day we asked mom again to quit drinking and she finally said yes. She had finally found out how to take care of us and love us even more. After about five years me and my brother Anthony wanted to go to the fall fair in September. Then she started to drink again for three whole weeks. After the three whole weeks we had a family talk and she asked what we wanted in the whole entire world. I said that we wanted for her to stop drinking and she stopped because she loves us.

Cherie Thomas
Port Alberni, BC

My Mother

My mother is outstanding,
she is a loving person
the only person who loves me.

My mother is protective,
she tells me from right or wrong
and says how life is so long.

My mother is strong,
she knows the words of praise
and knew a trail through a maze.

My mother is part of me.

Leanna Leon

Finding My Way

My name is Roberta Patrick. I am 18 years old. I belong to the Lake Babine Band and I also belong to the Frog Clan. I'm going to the Lakes District Secondary School. I'm in grade 11 and am working towards a career in the education field.

I look after 5 children at home during the evenings, they belong to my cousins (4 girls ages 9 months to 6 years) and my sister who is 1 year old. My work experience teacher found out I was good with children when he was checking out my poor attendance and suggested I might try out 6 weeks at a Primary School to see if I liked it.

I decided to work at Muriel Mould Primary School with the grade one students. I enjoy being around kids at the age of 7 and younger ones under the age of 7. I thought I could work with the grade ones, and give it a try.

I began working as a Teacher's Aid at Muriel Mould Primary School on October 18, 1994 for 6 weeks, 3 times a week, which was Tuesday, Wednesday and Thursday, up till Nov. 24, 1994. I enjoyed working there, it was wonderful. We all got along. I also had fun with the kids. As I worked with the grade one kids, at noon hours I would be the supervisor out on the play grounds.

In my job as a Teachers Aid, I was to help the teacher get a few things ready for the class. Like do some writings, some photocopying, mark the kids notebooks and help a few kids on their reading. I had 2 different classes to work with. One in the morning and one in the afternoon.

I'm writing this in case somebody else out there is having a hard time finding out where they can fit in the work world doing things they can already do well and get paid for it. Skills and things you do well, you may not even recognize because they come naturally to you, maybe extremely difficult or even impossible for others, so you have a natural skill or gift.

The academic work ahead of me now is sometimes scary but I plan to build up my work experience with my work experience teachers help and enter the NITEP (Native Indian Teacher Education Program). At UBC as a mature student, I have to work on my Math, Science and formal English skills to write a GED test for admission. It will take me 5 years to complete this, which seems like forever, but I know it's worth while, and I can help other people which makes me feel good about myself and my life.

I have been in Alternate Program for 2 years, then I got into regular classes in grade 9/10. Now I'm back in school. I have a very positive future ahead of me as long as I keep working towards it.

Sincerely

Roberta Patrick
Burns Lake, BC

What Does It Mean to be Native?

To some it means that they are proud,
    And these are ones who believe they are to be loud.
To others it means that they are ashamed,
    And these are the ones who believe they are blamed.
To some they feel that they are strong,
    These are the equals who think they are never wrong.
To the others they feel that they are weak,
    These are the equals that are scared to speak.
It means we will never live in freedom,
    Only to be seen uncivilized and dumb.
It means that soon we will be a forgotten race,
    Only to be lost in the Whiteman's grace.
It means we will learn to fight with each other,
    Because of jealous rage for our Sister and Brother.
It means you will not believe what is written here,
    Because it is the truth you mostly fear.

Roger Smith, age 18
Thompson Nation
Kamloops, BC

Trevor (Trey) Hunt, age 19, Kwakiutl Band, Port Hardy, BC

A mental Picture is all I have of you.

There are times I wish it would have been more,
    yet I understand.
Could you have understood the same?

I can't help but fear,
    where did things go wrong?
Was there doubt of things to be even better?

You said it had nothing to do with me,
    even though this was all between us.
Do you still feel you made the wrong choice?

It is said the moment will not last,
    but shall your memory of us last forever?
Do you feel there are memories worth looking back on?

I felt your emotions were mixed with fear,
    and I wish that you could have overcome this.
If not for me, then for yourself.

Prove your means. All people struggle,
    is this a lesson learned and to be lived by?
Was this a transition of emotion?

Try not to confuse yourself by listening to others,
    you should follow your heart, your true emotion.
Take what they say only into consideration.

Dee Derickson, age 18, grade 12
Okanagan Nation
Westbank, BC

Being With You

Being with you my friend
helps me to be strong.
Being with you, tells me I can do it.
Knowing you as the teacher of me
can make a difference.
Being with you, I can trust
Being with you, I get knowledge.

Murray Chief
Pitt Meadows, BC

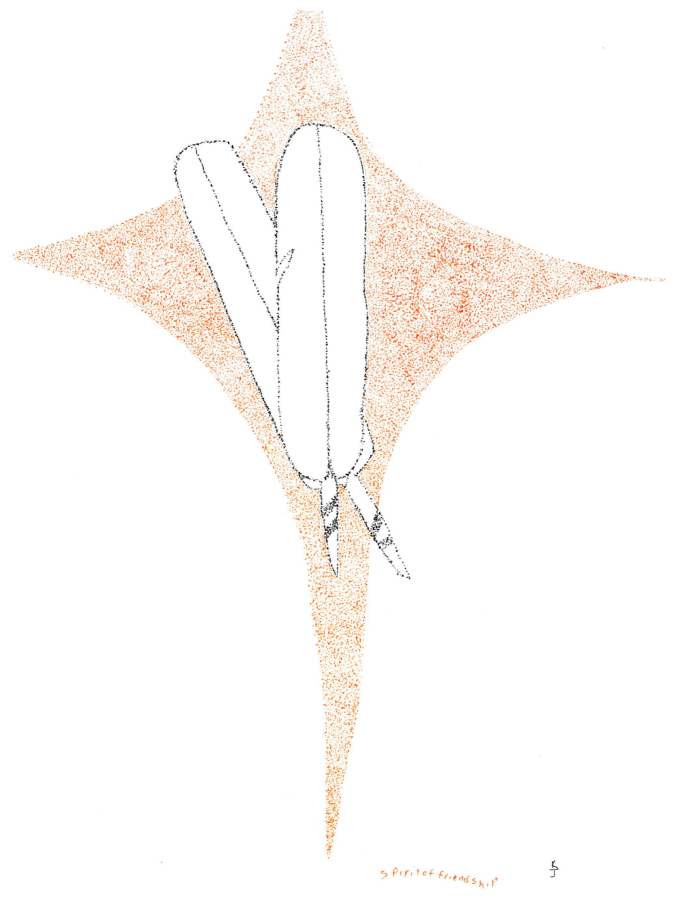

"Spirit of Friendship

In Life

It used to be fun but now I don't know
It was fun because all I had in my mind was succeeding
Reaching my goal in life, finishing school, but now I don't know
Life as I see it now is different,
I see no happiness, no excitement, no laughter
I seek other alternatives
I've tried other alternatives out of this time of my life.
Too many things in my mind, so many that my mind feels empty
Yet it's full, my mind, with the wrong stuff
Ignoring the things it used to use
Why now? Why here? why me?...
...I thought the world had come to an end
Everything that used to be fun became dangerous
Everyday became a risk of life or death
I wonder why I was set on this earth,
My problems got worse as I tried to find myself
Soon I didn't care about myself
Others would come to me
but I was too stubborn, I wished they would leave me alone
But they wouldn't go away
I started to think, they know something is wrong
I started to listen, and let it all out
I found the people who were trying the most
Were the ones that cared.

Dennis Moses Williams - age 15
Quatsino Band
Port Hardy, BC

Love

I would like you to know
How much you really hurt me.
You are hurting me deeply and
You don't even realize it.
Inch by inch, word by word
You are slowly tearing my insides apart.
It is really the simplest things but
Those simple things mean a great deal to me.
I want to spend as much time with you
As I can.
When I need you the most
You push me away the most.
Why is it always the opposite with the two of us?
Why can't we ever be there for one another
When in need the most!
I feel at the lowest point of life and
I don't know how much more neglect
I can take.
Why won't you understand me and
Take me seriously?!
"I LOVE YOU!"
These are very strong words for me to say and
I mean them very dearly.
I wanted to say them to you but
These words won't come out of my mouth but
Only through a pen on paper.
I wanted to say it before it was to late.
Perhaps, when I'm older
I will understand what your putting me through.
I just wanted you to know
How much you are hurting me

Ramona Smith
age 17, grade 12
Lytton First Nation
Lytton, BC

Rape

Rape
A kiss is not a contract,
A feel is not consent.
A hard-on doesn't give you
the right to force yourself
inside a woman.
Rape.
When your looks,
wit, styles, status,
personality, clothes,
cars, cash, dinners and
drinks, don't entice her
to have sex with you
will you use?
Rape.
When it happens to your
mother, daughter, friend,
sister, girlfriend, cousin,
niece, aunt, grandmother,
or wife, will you say,
she was asking for it?

Brian Michell, age 14, grade 8
Kanaka Bar Band
Lytton, BC

Closer By The River

As I walk close by the river
I think about the way I could
  bring things in front of me

As I walk closer and closer
someone comes from behind
  grabbing me with lust

Now thinking of the river
and the man who saved me
  brings me closer to life

Nicole Robert, age 15

MARY'S EYES

First thing you should know is that Mary wears glasses
They prove to shield emotions she doesn't want to see

Second thing is she is a strong proud Native woman with a strong heart
Everyone should know someone like her
Most do but don't recognize it when they meet her

Mary loves to have a good time and one will rarely see her without a smile
Her laughter is magic but to some it brings shame

When I first met her she smiled and laughed with an outstretched hand
I took her hand and felt comfort
The simple touch warmed me inside

After a nice friendly visit I rose to leave and took her hand once more
Only this time she pulled and spoke in my ear
"If you need someone to talk with or a place to stay, look for me"

In that short time Mary knew all about me
I thought I knew her as well, a kind understanding woman who's lived my life before me
The pain, the suffering, the searching for some kind of joy, any kind of joy

I found out later I was wrong
for when she thought no one could see she removed the shield before her eyes
and I no longer saw the joyous and proud woman I knew

I saw emotions
More than anything there was pain

So much pain I saw in her eyes I knew it couldn't belong only to her
It was my pain and countless others like me
all who had searched and found comfort in Mary, Mary was one of the few

The few that could understand and never blame
Never tell a young man he shouldn't have provided his parents
Never tell a young woman she was asking for it

Then I knew it was my turn and I approached her
I took her glasses for she would need them no more
and I held her and I comforted her and finally
I understood

Wendy Quinn, age 18, grade 12
Metis/Cree, Kelowna, BC

WHO KNOWS

EVERYONE
IS
A
CHILD
WHEN WE PLAY THESE GAMES OF EXCESS.
EVERYONE
IS
SAD
LIKE
ME, BEHIND THE GRINNING FACES AND STAINED YELLOW TEETH.
EVERYONE
PRETENDS
TO KNOW

Patrick James Haugen, age 17, grade 12
Lytton First Nation, Lytton, BC

Pumba stuck under a tree stump drawn by Cassy Watts

FRIENDS

FRIEND'S ARE PEOPLE WHO ARE ALWAYS THERE FOR YOU,
    WHEN YOU NEED THEM OR JUST TO LAUGH WITH.
FRIEND'S HAVE FUN, GOOF AROUND AND PLAY TOGETHER.
    FRIEND'S TREAT YOU NICE, WITH RESPECT, AND LOYALTY;
THEY ALSO EXPECT THE SAME IN RETURN.
    FRIEND'S DON'T PUT EACH OTHER DOWN OR LAUGH AT THEM,
FRIENDS RESPECT YOU FOR WHO YOU ARE, NOT WHAT YOU ARE.
    THAT'S WHAT FRIENDS ARE!

Cassie Adams, age 12, grade 8
Lytton First Nation
Lytton, BC

Untitled One

Why couldn't he tell her hi,
Why couldn't he talk to her.
When he saw her all he could
do was listen to his heart beat
faster as she walks by. She tells
him hi, all he could do was nod his
head trying to tell her hi.
She never talks to him again
all because he never told
her, he was shy.

Guy Archie
Canim Lake Band, 100 Mile House, BC

Untitled Two

As time goes by I think of you, where
did you go, will ever find you in this
giant world. I keep on looking without
a trace, looking for that one and only
face. I follow my heart as it cries
for you but will it ever find you in
this giant world.

Guy Archie
Canim Lake Band, 100 Mile House, BC

Our Futures......

My Future

I want to live at Sproat Lake in a house.
I want to get married and have four kids.
I want to have a family and be rich enough to feed my four kids.
I want to send my kids to College and University.
I want to be a manager of a video store because I like movies.
I want my kids to have a Native culture as well.
The culture is important because,
I want them to be smart and learn their own culture.
I want my life to be happy and nothing wrong or happen to my family.
I want my kids to have beautiful kids too.
I want my kids life to be like that too.

That's all I see in my future.

Catherine Fred, age 12
Port Alberni, BC

Look Into My Future

When I look into my future I'm worried because on the news they say all these bad things are supposed to be happening to the world like an earthquake, the earth exploding and some other stuff. Other than that, I think my life is going to be really good. I want to have two kids. Hopefully get a job as a Marine Biologist so I will get a pretty good paying job to feed and support my family. I want to finish school first. I don't want to be too rich or too poor. I just want to have enough money for school and my family. I would like to still keep my culture. I could talk to my kids in Indian. I could teach them how to draw, to dance and basket weave. These are the simple things I could do in the future.

Linsey Haggard
Age 10, grade 5
Port Alberni, BC

My Future

When I look into my future I see myself as a successful person.
I am going to be living in a house on the reserve. I want a normal house I can be comfortable in.
My transportation is going to be a car and a truck. My truck is going to be pretty big it has a super cab.
I am going to be living out on my own. Not with my parents
Money is not a big goal for me right now. But I realize that money will be important in my future.
"Coming of age potlatch"
I am going to a vocational school to a learn a trade. I would like to be a mechanic who works on boats.
I hope that when I come of age I can have a potlatch to celebrate. I would also like to keep my culture alive by showing the world what I know. I know some songs and dances and I can draw the way my people have done for many years.
When I look at the future I am happy about all the things I am going to do.

Vance Kyle Sieber
age 11
Port Alberni, BC

My Future

When I look into the future I see myself as a wife with two kids and a husband. In the future I am going to have a good education so I can pay bills and buy food and clothes for my children and husband. I hope my kids have a better future than I do. I also hope that my kids have a good education and pay their bills and act like a responsible adult. But if I don't have all those things I hope I can at least have a good education. In the future I want to be a Marine Biologist. A Marine Biologist studies about ocean life. In the future I might live with my family until I am old enough to be responsible. In the future I hope that my culture can be a part of my life. I can keep the culture alive by doing simple things I could tell stories to my children, teach my children dances and songs. I also like to draw. My pictures will show the world where I come from and who I am.

Brandee Sam
age 11, grade 5
Port Alberni, BC

My Future

When I look into my future I see me having a balanced life. This means I don't want to be too rich or too poor I want to have the freedom to do anything I want to do. The kind of job I want when I'm an adult is to be a doctor or lawyer. I want to be a doctor or lawyer because they make a lot of money. Then I would save up my money to buy a Lamborghini and a new house. My Lamborghini would be purple because purple is my favourite colour. Me and my family would live in the house because I love my family. If my family would be alive. I would buy them some of the stuff that they would want. When I'm almost an adult I am going to go to college and university to get my job. I'll have to go to university for seven years to become a doctor or lawyer. When I'm finished school I'll ask my mom and dad to have a potlatch for me. This would be important to me so when I'm older I could remember it. To me this would be a balanced life.

David Prest
age 11, grade 6
Port Alberni, BC

The Future

I don't think there is going to be a future for me because of my sickness. I might not be able to have a family, or a job. I might not even get to finish school. People always ask me how I'm doing they make it sound like I'm not even gonna reach twenty five. Some people treat me like a little kid. I try to tell them to stop treating me like a little kid but it's hard because they're my family. I can't be in the sun so that means that I can't go swimming as much as I used to. I pray every night and morning. Why won't it work? My family was great until we found out about my sickness. Now I have to go through a whole bunch of tests. I have to get blood tests every three months. My aunties won't tell me what kind of sickness. I guess they don't want to help find out what kind of sickness I have. I'm not saying I don't like them I just expected them to help out. And when I forget about my sickness somebody always has to go and talk about it right in front of me. Makes me feel stupid. It makes me feel like I want to cry. When my cousins tease me about my sickness that just makes me feel even worse. My Auntie Beep made me feel a lot better when she talked to me. And told me that she had a friend with the same sickness. I feel a little better now.

Mary Barney
age 12, grade 6
Port Alberni, BC

My Future

Sometimes I don't want to look into the future because the world might end. From all the pollution in the world. If there will be a world, I will go to college and university and become a doctor in Vancouver. When I get enough money and get a husband and have one child. I would have a really nice house. When the baby is born I will buy a blue van. When I am in Vancouver and rent a hall and have a potlatch with all my family in Vancouver. Then I will teach my child Native songs, dances, and drawings. I hope my kid won't grow up poor and steal or be a criminal. I also hope my child will not forget the things I tell him or her because I don't want the kid to make the same mistakes as I did. That's how I think my future will turn out.

Crissy Williams
Port Alberni, BC

My Future

In my future I see a lot of bright circles up in the sky.

In my future I see me have two kids and a bird for my kids to play with.

In my future I see me living in a big mansion with my kids.

In my future I see me being a police woman for my job.

In my future I see I'll have a lot of grandchildren.

In my future these are the circles I see.

Nancy Antoine
Port Alberni, BC

Tasha Oscar, Kelowna, BC

My Future

When I look into my future I think I want to be a doctor or a basketball player. I think I will be a basketball player. I will have two kids and a wife. I will be good to my kids. I will find a big house with a pool for my two kids and my wife. After I play basketball I will go straight home to my wife and kids. I will have a potlatch for my two kids. After they finish the potlatch I would have a party at my house. I never had a party. I would go to a fun centre with my kids if I got robbed I would feel so mad and my wife would be too — I think. Then if all my friends gave me some stuff I would feel better.

Anthony Mark
Port Alberni, BC

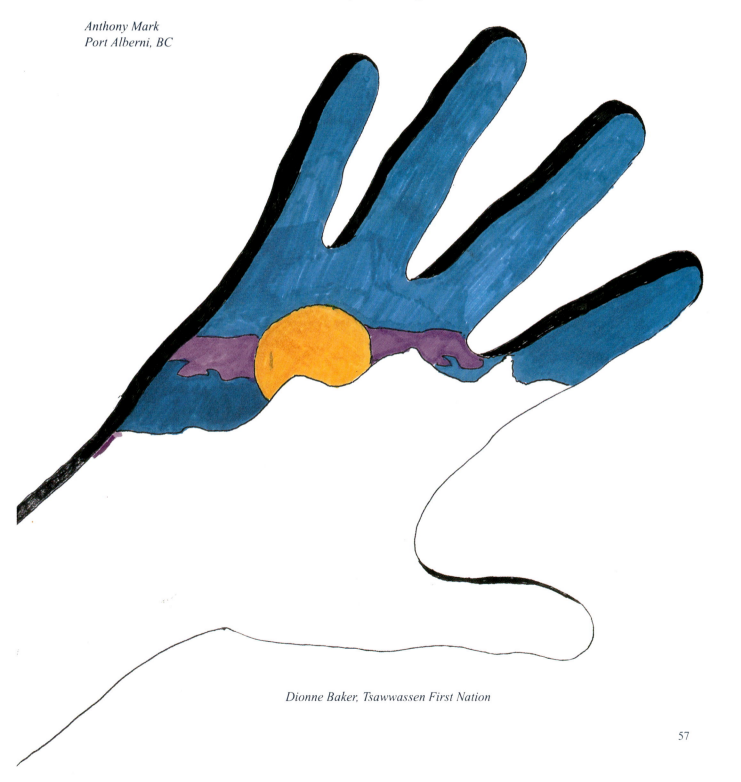

Dionne Baker, Tsawwassen First Nation

What's Down That Long Road Ahead?

As the road gets longer
The fear ahead grows on
What's that road going to bring me
Will I ever get through this road
Maybe someone I love so deeply, will leave me behind
And never turn around to pick me up again
Will I ever get to see the family I dream of
Or will I see my family/friends drown in tears
The road ahead of me will be unknown
This fear I fear so much
Will it tell me in my dreams
I shall walk this road to face these fears
Thou I'm frightened for my families in the days to come
Down that road there's something good
And there's something bad
But I can never overcome it.

Graylin Johnny
Age 16
Williams Lake, BC

Sun Shines

I am walking
through tall green grass.
It tickles
my legs and arms.
There
is the bright warm sun.
I sit under a tree.
It is cool there.
I smell the fresh scent
of flowers.
It is starting
to get dark.
I go inside
and hope for another day like this.

Jessica Michel, age 11, grade 6
Adams Lake Band

Mother Earth

Mother of great mystery,
where are you?
In my heart?
In my soul?
As a spirit that roams free?

You are the forgotten one,
one of many.
When the eagles cry,
is it you?

Mother of great mystery,
Where is the racing river?
Where once the clear waters flowed?
Is it covered in mankind?

May I ask,
What is your dream?
Is it to laugh and to cry?

I have so many questions to ask,
I wish you could answer,
but that's only because
you're the Mother of great mystery.

Leanne Gabriel, age 14
Okanagan Nation, Penticton, BC

JOURNEY OBSERVATIONS

The roads nearly bleed a sweaty river
with unbridled fear on a journey to plastic serenity
Love turns the heart into a soft callous,
perverted eyes hide in marshmallows,
the princess eats yogurt, licking her age spots
destiny for the young.
It will all come, in time he will come.
I slept in a dead body,
every breath a dream, every breath a whisper.
Still frozen in an enemy.
The lost never wake.
The evaluation of the path, a fading, meandering, memory only the blind
can guide.
A path of remorse and filth.
I buried my arms to my chest and my mind to the naked innocence of faithful fear.
Yogurt is bacteria.
The gardens are immortal.
Alive to survive in her box of secrets.
Old eyes, waking eyes.
Filthy brains need to breath,
need to breed.
Those glossy eyes and ethnic fingers scratch nearly but barely at the souls, soles of
shoes that is.
When does it end for the chronic yawners?
Rabbits feet.
"Always the promise of something better"
Always the promise of a funeral.
The flowers always die, everything remains dirty,
fossilized in dirt.
Where do the jewels go?
It's all commission in this world.
Unified with our lips, our eyes always closed,
big black curls, bitter tears.
Same journey, same road, same traffic.
Control the speed.
She could have been a vamp perhaps an ancient goddess.
Is a princess always royalty in the mirror? Or does the dye wash out
while the coach is in motion. One direction.
Breathing is prohibited on this journey.
I've already been here, I still can't breath but I can't leave, this
grave is generous.
The animals are free, unleashed and old, wrinkles and mold
but it was here when you arrived
Another developed machine in the process of escape.

Today we rest in the clouds, If the moon stares back does it make you a radiant reflection, or a deprived romantic with no justice to surrender, and no kiss to commend her.
My lips crumble the passengers minds.
Death the messenger of joy will arrive at the next exit.
Take me here again and I will show you mountains where the sun reveals scars. An hour from departure,
I ask is the novel always in fine print?,
Is there always an emergency exit?
Is there comfort in your sleep?

Charlene Dunstan
Lytton, BC

Untitled

In the visions of the silence
Motions in our moments pain
Words that speaks to emptiness
Humanities ignorance only vain
Listen as the earth weeps
As her tears make rivers flow
Waves that shore the silence
In the greed that we bestow
In the fragments of desire
Are we searching for love to weave?
Seemingly in the blindness
We await our souls to be deceived
Earths voice echoes in our ears
Tremors in the canyons silence
And the earth, with the river;
Will tidal a storm of tears.

Shayla Allison, age 18
Okanagan Nation, Oliver, BC

Givers of Life

I am as the mountains,
once powerful, weakening now.
I am losing my spirit,
as the mountains are losing their trees.
Givers of air.
Givers of life.

Robin Coble, age 14, grade 8
Okanagan Nation, Kelowna, BC

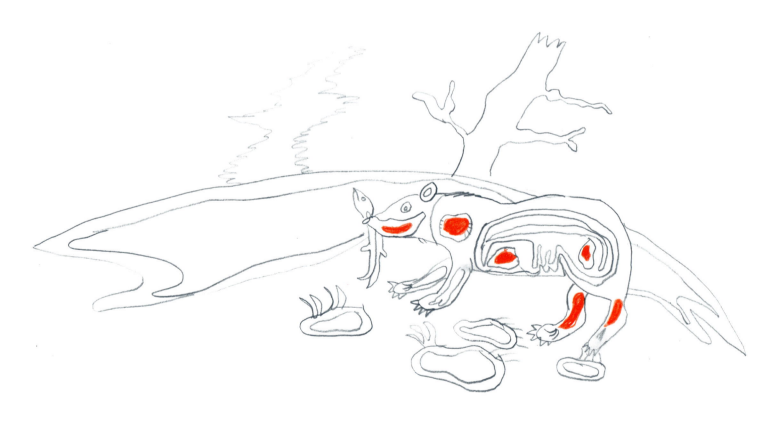

Artwork - Wayne Brown

A Rose

In it's crystal home.
With the smell of perfume.
With only the light of one candle.
The deep color of red
From bright to dull.
Still fills my heart with love.
The fullness has altered.
To the shrivel of it's death.
The beauty of life has faded.
Once living with vitality.
Now a symbol of a memory
I'll keep to the day I die.

Amy Francis
Maple Ridge, BC

Leukemia

My little brother
is like a rose
so delicate
and so fragile.
He cries for help
and anger fills me because
I can't help him.
His weeping is difficult
and sad to hear.

Ryan Hance
Ulkatcho, Anahim Lake

The Man in The Moon

Many moons ago the Native man was very happy. He had the buffalo herds roaming around and all sorts of fish in the lakes, rivers and oceans. He had the eagles and other birds flying high in the sky at all times, and the birds even woke him up early in the morning to take a mountain bath. The Native man even had clean water to drink right from the river or lake. The water he drank was crystal clear, he had the berries to pick and eat right off the bush. The salmon and buffalo provided tons of food, clothes and tools. The buffalo gave him nice warm leather. He could go out and fish anywhere he liked to.

Then the Native man noticed that the buffalo didn't come around anymore and the fish didn't swim in every lake, river, or ocean. All the waters even started to change colour. Then he noticed that the trees started to changed into square teepees or like Longhouses, only they weren't as long. The paths turned into grey rock with the colour of the big circle in the sky. Then his language slowly started to change. His leather started to change, it wasn't as warm as it used to be. The birds didn't wake him up anymore, and when he looked up, there was a black cloud. When he went to pick berries, there was nothing there but a man asking the Native man to give him furs to eat his own berries. Then the water started to come in a cone shaped object . . . only this water wasn't the same. It made his powerful dancing legs weak and made everything move by itself. It didn't taste the same either. The Native man started to like it more and more. It made him beat up his wife and children. It made him forget where he was the night before.

And elder told the Native man, "It is evil, give it up, it will put a spell on you and make you want it more. It will make you do more bad things." Then the elder told him to go somewhere and think of what he will do. So the Native man agreed, but he said he will not return until the animals, old good water, and the Native language come back. The Native man has been up there ever since.

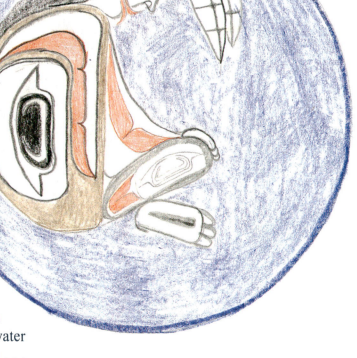

Wilfred George
age 17, grade 10
Coast Salish Nation
Victoria, BC

AN EAGLE SOARS

an eagle soars
an eagle soars like a dream or a goal
a goal for yourself or a dream for your people
a goal for yourself, to stop the abuse
the abuse of alcohol, racism, and fighting.
a dream for your people,
a dream of happiness, long love and a big family
like a dream or a goal an eagle always soars,
an eagle soars proud, big, high and flies with grace
to stop the abuse an eagle is big,
to set dreams an eagle flies high
stop the abuse set dream's plus goal's like an eagle that soars
. . . . an eagle soars.

Jay Millar
age 17, grade 10
Victoria, BC

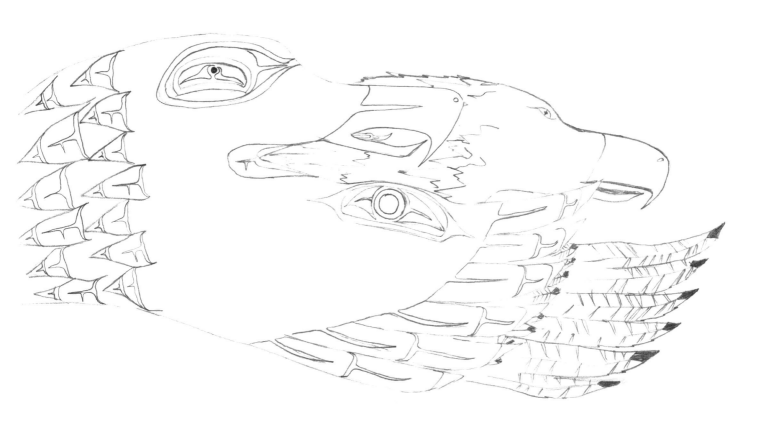

Artwork - Jay Millar

I want to be a Bird

I want to be a bird
I want to soar high above the sky
I want to stretch my wings across the world
With no regrets, no fear, and no pain
I want to release all the conflict of this terrible
world, and go into a world full of freedom and harmony
I want to be a bird
I want to run from my problems and
spread my wings
I want to touch the stars
and hear the angels cry out in happiness
I want the wind to touch my face
And the sun to warm my heart
If I was only a bird

Rosemaria Leamont
age 15. grade 9
Kelowna, BC

When Night Falls

I see the shadows
of the trees
I hear the wind
whistling
I look up at the moon
so bright
so calm and quiet
Watching the stars
and fall to sleep

Jessica Michel
age 11, grade 6
Adams Lake Band

By the dawn of day, the eagle spreads it's wings.

    Fly, fly

It flies through the deep blue skies, higher

than the clouds.

Where it can't be seen.

Murray Chief
Pitt Meadows, BC

THUNDERBIRD

Artwork - John Edward

I Am A Native

I am a Native.
I watch the town slowly get bigger and the pollution gets stronger. As the machines tear out the trees, there is one less breath in the air of the wilderness.

The eagles soar high above life in the air, the bears wander in the depth of the forest and the whales swim in the ocean waters. But for this to continue we have to do our part and do anything to slow down the pollution that is killing our culture and our land. We all like to see the early spring, mornings to night, but we don't like smelling all the smog.

But it's not only the human that doesn't like to smell it, or swim in it, it is also the animals, birds and fish that we all depend on as they depend on us.

We may get blamed for things that are their mistakes because it is not only Natives that fish or hunt, it is everybody.

We all have to understand to respect ourselves and also the land.

Miranda Lynn George
Age 14, grade 8/9
Coldwater Band, Merritt, BC

The Lady In Black

She is the lady of Darkness
The one who holds the rose
in her hand, and cries while she
remembers her lover who died last
spring: She wears the mask to hide
the pain of her memories of her
life on this earth. so she sits there
and cries while she stares out
into the darkness and holds the
rose in her hand.

Tyne Lomax
grade 10
Kelowna, BC

Artwork - Joyce Joseph, age 17, Kamloops, BC

The Past

This is my idea of how it would be in the past for our Native people.

In the olden days of 1389, Natives suffered, and died in battles against nature. They were in the mountains, with beautiful green grass fields, with beautiful flowers of spring.

There were birds such as the Eagle, Hawk etc. and animals, and roasting meat hanging off spears over the fire. Some people who couldn't start fires would eat red, raw, unhealthy meat. Thousands of people also risked their lives hunting and protecting against the animals, for their land and other peoples lives. Their hearts would break, when special people to the land, died.

Land shrivelled, people grew thinner, and nature began to die. Tee pees grew thin and cold. Winter came, people froze, and died a sorrowful, painful, sad death. A few survived, five men and five women, and then they had kids and their kids had kids. In centuries the culture grew bigger, but the air was getting badly polluted by the every day fires. These kind of people were nothing like those before them.

They worked really hard in the past to keep this planet healthy. Natives were the first kind of people to discover Canada. The native people started fire. The trees Western Red Cedar, Hemlock, and Pine trees help all of Human kind to breathe fresh air. Native culture is still growing today. All the great hunters are dead, and will not be forgotten, and hopefully never will.

100 years in the future (in 1489), a new baby was born with the name of Eric Wilson. He grew up on a beautiful healthy reserve. When he was a teenager he ran for chief. The elders, kids, and basically the whole reserve voted for him.

He began to be chief year after year. His parents died when he was 30 years old. In the future, he would now be an elder, and the kids grew into adults. By this time when the kids finally learned to hunt for huge bears, these bears hadn't been fed in weeks. Later, the chief dies, the Europeans come, a jumbo war begins, they choose to get along. Here we are now.

Eric Wilson, age 10
Homalco Band
Port Alberni, BC

Clint Donald, Sewepemc Nation, Kamloops, BC

Freedom

Eagles roam the sky
Fly through the air gracefully
Looking for mice
Feathers flowing with the wind
Freedom for the Indians

Quinten Jack
Redstone
Williams Lake, BC

Kodiak Lunch

Hungry Kodiak
Stares at the spawning salmon
From the river bank
Chomping, ripping them apart
Delicious in his mouth.

Bradley Johnson
Alkali
Williams lake, BC

Sonnet To My People

Nature's way is free in my soul
The thrill of dancing and drumming
Listening to the rhythmic chanting.
They can always fill up your bowl,
Spirits can always take control,
You feel so proud to be singing,
Making sure elders are smiling,
Can't come down when you are aglow.

The others didn't like our pride.
They liked my ancestors to hide
Our culture and dances were banned.
Sometimes they couldn't even stand
Their harassment and being wrong
We still live culture that is strong.

Tanya Stump
Anaham
Williams Lake, Bc

Dawn

Young deer standing proud
In mist of the morning sun
Standing with the herd.

Bradley Johnson
Alkali
Williams Lake, BC

Thunder

Bison walking the earth
Huge giants thundered the ground
They travelled in herds
We ran them off the high cliff
Winter food for our families.

Ryan Hance
Anaham
Williams Lake, BC

Stars

As I gaze upon the stars
I may see the life
before me with happiness

Even before I got a chance
I see my future
I flash back to the end

Ending of my life came
with fear inside
of the lies that I said

Nicole Robert
age 15

Back Home Again

I am back home again,
trekking across the prairie.
Moccasins upon my feet
and a buckskin dress
upon my body

He walks beside me,
tall and handsome. His long, black hair
flowing over his well tanned back,
with a beautiful spotted eagle feather
bobbing up and down
with each new step.

His shining black eyes
seem to dance and laugh
as those of a young child.
He flashes me a knowing glance
and smile,
as if to say how much he loves me.

He knows as well as I
that we are bound
by heart and soul
till the end of time.
He knows as well as I
that I am his
and he is mine.

I hold his hand in mine,
and admire his perfection.
His soft red skin
is the colour of Mother Earth,
signifying his pureness

He is a strong, brave warrior
among our people,
and a handsome, loving husband
to me.
Although he may be young
in years,
he is more of a man
than many will be.

I am back home again,
trekking across the prairie,
his hand in mine
my heart in his.

Mikelle Sasaskamoose, Ahtakakoop, Cree Nation, Kamloops, BC

Journals — Through the Eyes of My People

Early Spring

When I stand there and watch these big,
What they call ships float in, I think of,
What do they bring now
My mind is filled with all sorts of questions
As these unfamiliar faces come off the ship
Plagued with foreign diseases.
All I could do is stand there and ponder
About the rest of my people, my family.

Mid Spring

When I see these people destroying our land
Up and down the rivers only one thing comes to mind,
Why are they doing this
My people are slowly losing land and
Many do not realize it yet,
How long will this go on before anyone knows what
Values are being lost

Mid Spring

Everyday as I walk along our land
I see my people slowly going through various changes.
They got something different in their hands
Everyday while others got something else,
A disease that slowly spreads but
Seems to be killing fast.

Late Spring

When I see all my people dying rapidly of
An unknown plague,
I fear for my family who is also slowly
Infested by disease. These people come to
My country in hope to rapidly improve their future,
While slowly destroying ours.
Why do these people risk such a great journey
To ruin the lives of one race of people?
I feel this question will rise for many generations to come.

Early Summer

Now days my people are looking more confused.
I noticed that these people are literally putting

My people on certain plots of land to live, why
Everyday my family grows weaker and food is lesser,
These people are driving all our food, the game,
Further into the forests and away from us.
If this continues, how will our people survive
Through the rest of the seasons

Mid Summer

It's well into the summer now and
Things aren't improving at all.
Some of the animals are being trapped
For the price of their coats and nothing more.
I see that most of our food that falls into
The hands of these people goes mostly to waste
With little concern to them.

Late Summer

I can sense fall will be coming soon and
My family grows fewer and I feel illness
Trying to take my soul.
Most of my people have left now and
I think we will be stuck here till the end of our time.
Almost everyday I see a death,
If it isn't one of my people it's one of them.
No one has to live like this.

Early Winter

The days are shorter now, nights are longer, colder,
And the people of both races are much effected
From various health problems.
I still see these people fighting over our land,
Our food, what for? Do they not know the meaning of share
Sometimes I think that these people thrive on
The death of our land, our people,
But do not realize the destruction
They have done to themselves.

Mid Winter

I feel that winter has come to its peak now and
I miss the company of my family more than ever.
I have not been outside for days now.
I feel weaker like never before.
I lay here and think far back to what
Great damage that has been caused

Not only to us but to our land.
They have stripped much our cultural life
As well as from their own race,
They limited everyone to our land and food,
Even themselves,
They have plagued everyone throughout the land
And is now taking me.
I hope these people will pay back
One way or another for what they have taken.
I only wish that I could be here to see all this come......

Clint Donald, age 19
Sewepemc Nation, Kamloops, BC

Just a Grass Dancer's Tale

I see the people for only a second,
I hear the speakers for only two beats
Then I am gone I reckon
To a place where the spirit world meets
I see only one person
Standing always in front of me
She stands in buckskin, she is my hon.
And when I look at her I am free
I have no problems, no fears,
Nothing to take my mind off my task,
No cracking speakers, no loud cheers.
I know they are there, just behind a mask,
I don't know when there is a check beat
Or when it speeds up, but I hit them,
It is not my mind, it is my feet,
No it is my heart. But there is a problem,
there is something on the ground, that doesn't belong
So I must take it away
And give it to the owner among
The spirits here today.
But I don't know how to do this,
I've done it before
So again I'll let a spirit who will not miss
To use me as a door
To this world to take it back,
And as a spirit approaches I hear a whistle,
But no dancer surrounds the drumming pack,
Instead charge at me one at a time, as though a missile.

Roger Smith, age 17, Kamloops, BC

Artwork - Ray Zamara, age 11, grade 7, Lytton, BC

Colours

What is it like living as a colour?
White, yellow, black, red
Take your pick,
White seems best
I'm red, so they say
I look more brown
to me
but why should I care

There's no difference
That I can see
But no one really
Listens
Some would say
I'm a minority
I think I'm
A majority
No...I don't think
I'm a majority
That would be wrong
That would be stooping to the level of some
People who
like to put labels on things...people.

Robert (Bob) Wallas
Grade 11, Age 17
Quatsino Band
Port Hardy, BC

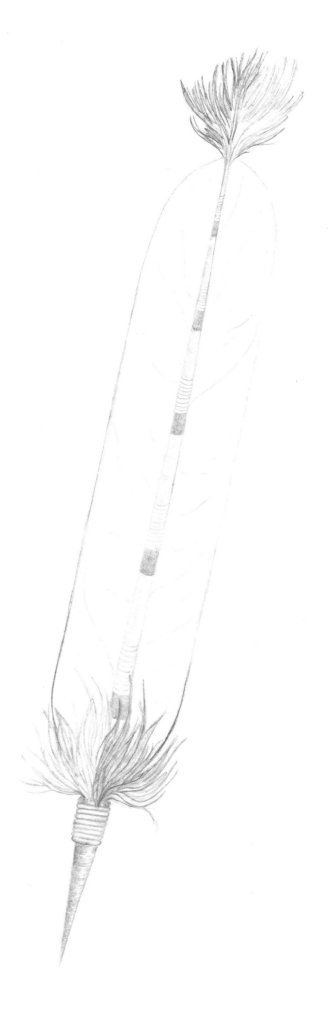

Quit It

Go away
You're not wanted
"Stop bugging me"
Leave me alone!
"Quit It"

Why am I so different to you?
Why do you treat me different from others?
Why do you bug me?
Why can't you think how I feel?
So just quit it!

Fawn Garcia
Age 15, Grade 10
Siska Band
Lytton, BC

Journal No. 9

your touch is blue
your breath is mine to feel
I can see through you though
but I can't feel
I wonder about the golden stream inside of you
but yet
I wonder within if it is for real
I throw my self to see if you would catch
I'm left flying in a black hole
Still to wonder
If
You are mine yet
I know but yet I don't
I only see what I know and then it's gone to me
your getting to me
you are the only one I want
your heart, read beating inside of you and you don't know
I know
I know
come to me and I'll tell you
I'll show the edge of life
You are forever mine

Dionne Baker, Tsawwassen First Nation, Delta, BC

The Flight

The day is gloomy and dark,
As any other day.
I get up and open the curtains,
All I can see, is mostly rain.
I go to school as am required to do.
I often wonder why I am living to learn of one society.
Why does one race has to do as one race wants.
Since the days of perfect society.
These were the days were everyone knew what they had to do
to survive.
When the leaders seen wrong, and placed it in history.
When the leaders saw suffering, and tried to heal it,
But war, destroyed it!
When the natives were taken and stuffed in schools,
Only to be forced to be given a white name.
Only to be forced to not remember the culture that we almost lost
Only to live by the approval of others,
And only to see the food, property and jewellery taken away
Now we are declared liars of the dark,
Now we need permission from a minister to make a decision
One society says we are a democratic society,
But I live in a dictating world.
Why should we listen to the commands of others,
Why should we be forced to live another life,
And why shouldn't we be allowed to own any land,
Countless items we mention fact,
Try to say belief is a belief,
and belief is fiction.
Try to say the facts,
because a fact is a fact,
and fact is reality.
Now the only choice of survival is to contribute to each other
We live on a labelled reserved.
Most think we own but we do not.
Hey the truth hurts.
All we meant was peace,
But the minority power dared to destroy us, as if we were
paper

David Watts
Nuu-chah-nulth Nation
Port Alberni, BC

Cam Gabriel. age 17, grade 10, Okanagan Nation, Penticton, BC

People staring and giving dirty looks
Talking loud enough to hear
But not for anyone else
Name calling
Rumours
Do you get used to it?
Does anyone?
Never thought it would hurt you,
Didn't think it was a big deal
until I got to know you.

Lola Camille,
age 19
Shuswap Nation, Savonna, BC

First Nations Youth & Canada's Drug Strategy

Throughout the last year, First Nations youth have been planning, coordinating and developing programs in conjunction with the Canada Drug Strategy Program, to not only use their time in a positive way, but also to provide programs that educate and inspire their peers and generations to follow. The youth have the power to pave the road to their future and they are using that power. This is made possible through the Canada Drug Strategy Program. A program that was set up to provide opportunity for youth to take control of their lives and create their own futures.

From the initiation of the Canada Drug Strategy program, youth from across the country have taken the initiative to create programs for themselves as alternatives to substance use and abuse. First Nations youth have coordinated workshops, field trips, sport festivals and various other activities to include themselves and others in a drug and alcohol free environments. This publication documents some of those activities as an incentive and informative collection of activities that can be enjoyed without the use of drugs and alcohol.

This program has proved to be successful in terms of innovative activities and learning experiences. Through this program, many First Nations youth will continue to live in a healthy, drug and alcohol free life style. They have learned that life is good and rewarding without the use of drugs and alcohol as well as some very useful skills that will contribute to a positive future.

It is through the Canada Drug Strategy Program that this publication is made possible. The En'owkin Centre of Penticton, BC, has produced this publication as an alternative to substance abuse and an opportunity for the First Nations youth of British Columbia to share their thoughts and talent with others, not only as an alternative, but as an incentive to others to use their talents to express themselves. It has been the mandate of this project to encourage the youth to talk about themselves and their lives. Not only the positive aspects, but all the issues that affect them as First Nations people and youth.

The first section of this book tells their stories and reflects their lives, dreams and aspirations. The second section briefly describes some of the programs that have occurred throughout the last year as Canada Drug Strategy initiatives and the third section provides them with a resource listing of agencies available to them. This is the second publication of the series and the En'owkin Centre is very proud to be a part of this documentation. As an educational institute, we strive to provide educational opportunity to all First Nations people for generations to come.

Border Artwork Courtesy of Gunargie O'Sullivan, Nimpkish Band, Alert Bay, BC

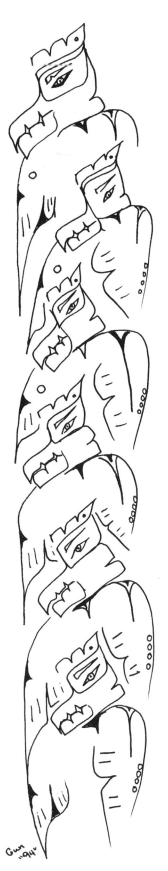

Aboriginal Sports/Recreation Association of B.C.

In 1994, the Aboriginal Sports/Recreation Association of B.C., hosted a *Aboriginal Provincial Youth Sportfestival*. The festival proved to be so successful, that they hosted another in March of 1995. This organization coordinated events for Aboriginal youth from the ages 13 to 19 and it was estimated that 800 youth from throughout the province would participate in the festival.

The goals of the Sportfestival were to promote addictions free lifestyles, foster self development, personal pride and enjoyment through sport recreation and cultural activities. The festival is also very helpful in providing a forum for youth to build networks throughout the province. The Association believes that sports, recreation and culture can be effectively used as an instrument of positive social interaction and change, such as countering alcohol and drug abuse.

The festival included sport activities as well as workshops targeting the youth. The workshops focused on personal development, AIDS awareness, career opportunities, suicide prevention and goal setting. The sport activities included volleyball, floor-hockey, indoor soccer, basketball and swimming. Also available to the youth were cultural activities and traditional sports.

Alexis Creek Band

The youth from the Alexis Creek Band were interested in learning traditional Native dancing. Together they decided that learning this part of their culture was fun as well as an activity in which they could learn more about their cultural heritage. The group was also involved with making their own traditional costumes. They learned how to make their traditional clothing, moccasins and hair accessories, using ideas from their Elders. The group made their own drums using deer and moose hides. The process involved in preparing their own costumes taught them useful skills and promoted self-esteem and self worth. The group conducted their own research in traditional design and consulted with other Native dance groups, drummers and singers. The intention of the group was to promote cultural awareness through Native dancing as a healthy drug and alcohol free activity. After preparing their costumes and learning dancing skills, the group was very interested in competing in pow-wows and organizing a pow-wow of their own to awaken the cultural spirit of their people and show the younger people how activities can be fun without the use of drugs and alcohol.

Anaham Indian Band

A group of ten youth organized a project entitled: *"Walking the Red Road" Youth of the 90's Alcohol and Drug Free.* The objective of the project was to create awareness, and facilitate prevention of drug and alcohol use. A series of workshops were organized for the youth to discuss issues that affected them. Workshop topics included; self-esteem, personal growth, suicide intervention/prevention, the medicine wheel and wholistic healing. The local Family Care Worker and the NNADAP Worker were active in facilitating workshops and gave lectures on topics that the youth felt were necessary. Role models were also invited to speak to the youth about their lives and experiences.

The objective of this series of workshops was to promote a healthier life style within the community, build self esteem and self actualization. The youth also learned, through the workshop process, a number of life skills such as career awareness, cultural and spiritual awareness. Activities of this nature are very important as a resource for youth and are helpful in fostering awareness concerning the issues that affect them as young Native people.

Chehalis Band

The Chehalis youth group coordinated a *Drug and Alcohol Awareness Youth Camp* for youth ages 13 to 19. The group coordinated a series of events that ran through the summer, as well as an exchange program with the Sechalt band. Forty youth from Chehalis travelled to Sechalt for two weeks to share their culture with the Sechalt band. The RCMP boats picked up the youth and took them to a isolated island where the youth were to stay for a two week period. The objective of this exercise was to isolate the youth from their regular daily activities and teach them important cultural and spiritual values as well as the traditional way of life. Activities on the island included, medicine walks, story telling and Sla-hal, a traditional stick game. The youth were taught the meaning of the game as well as how the game was relevant to the traditional way of life.

Other activities through the summer included a canoe trip, where 15 youth canoed from Chehalis to Scowlitz, a fish camp, where the Elders taught the youth how to fish, preserve and can the fish. The group participated in the spirit camp where 30 youth got involved in a medicine walk and story telling sessions from the Elders. An important activity that came out of this summer experience was the youth's contribution to the "meals on wheels" and the "wheels to meals" programs. The youth were very active in supplying salmon for the Elders of the community and contributing to the preserved food collection for the community.

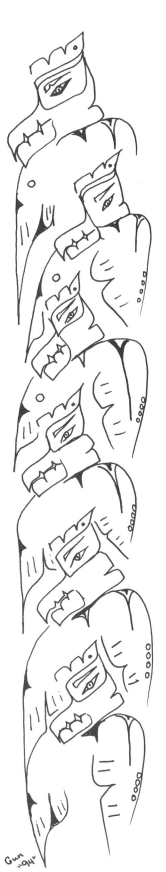

Kitsumkalum Band

The youth group from Kitsumkalum conducted six weeks of varied workshops to inform youth on the dangers and consequences of their actions. The workshops were conducted by a number of local people and the Elders were an active part of the process. The group learned life skills as part of the program as well as other skills that could assist them with in solving and dealing with issues that affect them. A group of youth went to a fishing camp as part of their wilderness training, as well as a trip to the Mills Memorial Hospital. At the hospital, the group visited the psychiatric ward and learned about what brings people to the ward and how they are helped. The youth also visited the local jail and an officer took them through and explained the policing system to them. The group also visited the Kitwanga Treatment Centre where they were made aware of drug and alcohol addictions and how these addictions can control and destroy their lives. The youth group were informed about some very important health issues like abortion, AIDS, STD's, and Herpes. They were given lectures on prevention as well as what certain drugs like, nicotine, alcohol, cocaine and marijuana do to their bodies. The group had a very busy six weeks and came through as more informed youth.

Lax Kw'alaams Band

The youth from Lax Kw'alaams coordinated a series of workshops to create awareness in drugs and alcohol abuse. The youth scheduled workshops where current videos, that focused on what drugs and alcohol does to the body, were shown and discussed. The videos included; *Journey to Recovery, Consequences of Drugs* and *Alcohol and Teenage Drinking and Drug Use*. The group also purchased a series of books that were informative on the effects of drugs and alcohol and made these books available to the youth on a lend basis. The objective of these workshops, books and videos was to show the youth that they can be responsible and say no to alcohol and drugs. The youth worked together with the older people of the community to achieve their goals.

Lower Kootenay Band

Four youth from the Lower Kootenay band attended a Youth Conference in Edmonton, Alberta. The youth gathered information and ideas to assist them in developing and organizing a youth group in their community. From the information they gathered at the conference, the group formed a *Young /Adult Support Group* that meets on a weekly basis. The group coordinated a sharing/healing circle that all local youth were invited to join. The objective of forming the circle was to give the youth an opportunity to share and talk about issues that concerned them. The circle was very productive in terms of resolving some of the problems that plague them as well as showing the younger people that there was an outlet available to them.

Nanaimo Band

The Nanaimo First Nations Youth Council coordinated a project where thirty of their youth could attend two Aboriginal Youth Conferences. They wanted to attend the *Dreamcatcher's Conference* in Edmonton, Alberta as well as the *National Addiction Awareness Week Conference* held in Crofton, BC. The youth attended the conference to learn more about drug and alcohol problems and to have some clean, healthy fun. The group also wanted to extend their knowledge in drug and alcohol addiction, prevention, coping skills, suicide prevention, AIDS/HIV awareness and personal skills like public speaking and proposal writing. Not only did the group want to learn these skills for themselves but to use them to help and share with other youth from their community. They wanted a better understanding of the function of youth in the community as role models and future leaders. Also, the youth council received support from their Chief and Council through an "open-door" policy for youth and support in their decision making process. The youth also hosted activities that other members of the community could get involved in such as the "Elder's Dinners" and other community based projects. The Nanaimo Youth Council was very active in the community and Council, and learned a number of valuable skills that assisted them, as well as other youth in the community. They acquired better communication skills, the ability to make better decisions and raised a higher profile in the community as responsible contributors.

Takla Lake Band

The youth from the Takla Lake Band were interested in learning skills which could supply them with the knowledge necessary to be better leaders in their community. The group believed that leadership follows confidence and confidence follows knowledge. To obtain this knowledge, the youth coordinated a series of workshops and practical experience situations. A workshop in Public Speaking was held to strengthen communication skills and self-confidence. A winter field trip was organized to teach the youth some basic survival skills and broaden their cultural knowledge. The youth learned to construct their own snowshoes and were taught the basics of trapping. A three day workshop consisting of Native dancing and beading techniques. The workshop included instruction on the art of Native dancing, preparing the regalia and beading techniques. The youth also participated in the *Youth Path Conference* in San Diego, California. The conference provided skill building workshops addressing topics such as, self-esteem enhancement, healthy Lifestyles, gang violence prevention and leadership training. Some of the youth attended a workshop in Edmonton, Alberta, that offered a series of youth oriented workshops including; *AIDS, Growing up in the Foster Care System, Developing a Balanced Relationship Between Native and Non-Native People, Independent Living Skills* and *Life Skills for Youth*. The youth who participated were successful in obtaining skills to assist them in being a leader in their community.

Taku River Tlingits Band

A group of 17 youth from the Taku River Tlingit First Nations raised funds to attend a pow-wow in Vancouver, and conduct a pow-wow workshop on their return. The objective of the excursion was to increase their awareness of other Native cultures and in turn increase the awareness of the community of the importance of culture. The youth were keen on learning more about their own culture and themselves. The youth also sought to enhance cross-cultural awareness through the participation of non-Native members of the community. Working as a group on this project, the youth also learned to better communicate and listen to other members of the community. Other important skills were learned through organizing the trip and raising money; they learned organizational skills, using computers and other office equipment, putting together a proposal and working as a team towards a common goal. At the pow-wow, the group had an opportunity to share their culture with other Native groups. This experience was very enlightening for all the youth involved.

West Moberly Band

The Spirit Wind Youth Group is comprised of members from the Saulteau and West Moberly First Nations. The group has 33 members ranging from age 12 to 25 years. The group was formed two years ago to create positive activities for youth of the two bands. The group has a Chief and four Councillors. The group coordinated a series of activities under the name – *With the Four Directions Comes Knowledge*, with the objective of building a better relationship within the community, learn Cree, their traditional language and establish a drug and alcohol free environment. The youth were also interested in developing better skills in communication and building positive self-identity.

An Elder/Youth gathering was organized to meet with the Elders and learn more about their traditional heritage and language. The group met twice monthly. Cree lessons with a community member were conducted twice a week to any youth that were interested. To ensure that the youngest members of the bands were included, a childrens fun day was organized where the young people could get involved with outdoor activities and the older youth.

First Nations Resource List

British Columbia Friendship Centres

B.C. Association of Friendship Centres
3-2475 Newton X Road
Saanichton, B.C. V0S 1M0
(604) 652-0210
Fax: 652-3102

Caribou Friendship Society
99-3rd Avenue South
Williams Lake, B.C. V2G 1J1
(604) 398-6831
Fax: 398-6115

Central Okanagan Indian Friendship Society
442 Leon Avenue
Kelowna, B.C. V1Y 6J3
Fax: 861-5514
(604) 763-4905

Conayt Friendship Society
P.O. Box 1989
2067 Quilchena Avenue
Merritt, B.C. V0K 2B0
(604) 378-5107
Fax: 378-6676

Dze'l K'ant Indian Friendship Society
P.O. Box 2920
3955 Third Avenue
Smithers, B.C. V0J 2N0
(604) 847-5211
Fax: 847-5144

Fort Nelson/Liard Native Friendship Society
Box 1266
5012-49th Avenue
Fort Nelson, B.C. V0C 1R0
(604) 774-2993
Fax: 774-2998

Friendship House Association
Box 512
744 Fraser Street
Prince Rupert, B.C. V8J 3R5
(604) 627-1717
Fax: 627-7533

Interior Indian Friendship Society
125 Palm Street
Kamloops, B.C. V2B 8J7
(604) 376-1296
Fax: 376-2275

Keeginaw Friendship Centre
10208-95th Avenue
Fort St. John, B.C. V1J 1J2
(604) 785-8566
Fax: 785-1507

Kermode Friendship Centre
3313 Kalum Street
Terrace, B.C. V8G 2N7
Fax: 635-3013
(604) 635-4906

Lillooet Friendship Society
Box 1270
357 Main Street
Lillooet, B.C. V0K 1V0
(604) 256-4146
Fax: 256-7928

Louis Riel Metis Council
207-13638 Grosvenor Road
Surrey, B.C. V3R 5C9
(604) 581-2522
Fax: 582-4820

Mission Indian Friendship Centre
33150 A-First Avenue
Mission, B.C. V2V 1G4
(604) 826-1281
Fax 826-4056

Nawican Friendship Centre
Box 593
1320-1-2nd Avenue
Dawson Creek, B.C. V1G 4H4
(604) 782-5202
Fax: 782-8411

Port Alberni Friendship Centre
3555-4th Avenue
P.O. Box 43
Port Alberni, B.C. V9Y 4H3
(604) 723-8281
Fax: 723-1877

Prince George Native Friendship Centre
144 George Street
Prince George, B.C. V2L 1P9
(604) 564-3568
Fax: 563-0924

Quesnel Tillicum Society Friendship Centre
319 North Fraser Drive
Quesnel, B.C. V2J 1Y8
(604) 992-8347
Fax: 992-5708

Tansi Friendship Centre Society
Box 418
4801 South Access Road
Chetwynd, B.C. V0C 1J0
(604) 788-2996
Fax: 788-2353

Tillicum Haus Society
927 Haliburton Avenue
Nanaimo, B.C. V9R 5K1
(604) 753-8291
Fax: 753-6560

United Native Nations Friendship Centre
2902-29th Avenue
Vernon, B.C. V1T 1Y7
(604) 542-1247
Fax: 542-3707

Valley Native Friendship Centre Society
Box 1015
462 Trans Canada Highway
Duncan, B.C. V9L 3Y2
(604) 748-2242
Fax: 748-2238

Vancouver Aboriginal Friendship Centre
1607 East Hastings Street
Vancouver, B.C. V5L 1S7
(604) 251-4844
Fax: 251-1986

Victoria Native Friendship Centre
533 Yates Street, Penthouse
Victoria, B.C. V8W 1K7
(604) 384-3211
Fax: 384-1586

First Nations Health Institutions & Authorities

Allied Indian Metis Association
2716 Clark Drive
Vancouver, B.C. V5T 2H2
(604) 874-9610

Anaham Reserve Health Program
Box 88
Alexis Creek, B.C. V0L 1A0
(604) 394-4342

Kakawis Family Development Centre
Meares Island
Box 17
Tofino, B.C. V0R 2Z0
(604) 725-3951

Kincolith First Nation Health Authorities
General Delivery
Kincolith, B.C. V0V 1B0
(604) 326-4212

Kitamaat Alcohol Abuse Program
Kitamaat Village Council
Haisla P.O. Box 1101
Kitamaat Village, B.C. V0T 2B0
(604) 639-9361

Lakalzap Health Clinic
Greenville, B.C. V0J 1X0
(604) 621-3274

Mount Currie Health Centre
P.O. Box 165
Mount Currie, B.C. V0N 2K0
(604) 894-6656

Nanaimo Indian Health Centre
1145 Totem Road
Nanaimo, B.C. V9R 1H1
(604) 753-9153/3481

Nimpkish Health Centre
P.O. Box 290
Alert Bay, B.C. V0N 1A0
(604) 974-5522

Nisga'a Valley Health Board Society
P.O. Box 234-256 Tait Avenue
New Aiyanish, B.C. V0J 1A0
(604) 633-2212

Nuu-cha-nulth Health Board
Box 1280
500 Mission Road
Port Alberni, B.C. V9Y 7M2
(604) 723-1223
Fax: 723-0463

Nuxalk Health Clinic
Box 93
Bella Coola, B.C. V0T 1C0
(604) 799-5441

Okanagan Self Help Project
Okanagan Indian Band
R.R. #7, Comp. 20, Site 8
Vernon, B.C. V1T 7Z3
(604) 542-4328

Red Road Warriors
AA Meetings for First Nations
Crabtree Corner
101 East Cordova Street
Vancouver, B.C. V6A 1K7

Tsartlip Health Centre
P.O. Box 70
Brentwood Bay, B.C. V0S 1A0
(604) 652-4473

Tsawout Health Centre
1210 Totem Lane
Sidney, B.C. V8L 5S4
(604) 652-1149

Vancouver Native Health Society
449 East Hastings
Vancouver, B.C. V6A 1P5
(604) 254-9949
Fax: 254-9948

Wilp Haldakws Gitwinksihlkw Health Centre
Box 48
Gitwinksihlkw, B.C. V0J 3T0
(604) 633-2611

Substance Abuse Centres

A.I.D.S. Prevention Program
1095 3rd Avenue
Prince George, B.C. V2L 1P9
(604) 564-1727

Alkali Drug and Alcohol Program
Alkali Lake Band Administration Office
Box 4479
Alkali Lake, B.C. V2G 2V5
(604) 440-5611

Bonaparte First Nation NNADAP
Box 669
Cache Creek, B.C. V0K 1H0
(604) 457-9624

Broman Lake First Nation NNADAP
Carrier-Sekani Tribal Council
Box 760
Burns Lake, B.C. V0J 1E0
(604) 698-7330-

Canim Lake Alcohol & Drug Abuse Program
Canim Lake Indian Band
P.O Box 1030
100 Mile House, B.C. V0K 2E0
(604) 397-2227

Caribou Friendship Society NNADAP
99 S-3rd Avenue
Williams Lake, B.C. V2G 1J1
(604) 398-6831

Chehalis Alcohol Counselling Service
Chehalis Indian Band
R.R. #1, Comp. 66, Chehalis Road
Agassiz, B.C. V0M 1A0
(604) 796-2116

Cheslatta Indian Band NNADAP
P.O. Box 909
Burns Lake, B.C. V0J 2E0
(604) 694-3363

Cowichan First Nation Council NNADAP
203 - 262 Station Street
Duncan, B.C. V9L 1N1
(604) 748-3196

Dease River Band Alcohol & Drug Program
General Delivery
Good Hope Lake, B.C. V0C 2Z0
(604) 239-3005

Drug & Alcohol Abuse Counselling Program
Sto:lo Nation - Canada
Box 280
Sardis, B.C. V2R 1A6
(604) 858-0662

Fountain First Nations NNADAP
Box 1330
Lillooet, B.C. V0K 1V0
(604) 256-4227

Gitsegukla Band Council NNADAP
36 Cascade Avenue R.R. #1
South Hazelton, B.C. V0J 2R0
(604) 849-5595

Gitwangak Band Council NNADAP
P.O. Box 400
Kitwanga, B.C. V0J 2A0
(604) 949-8343

Hartley Band Alcohol Program NNADAP
Trutch Channel
Hartley Bay, B.C. V1A 1A0
N692939

Heiltsuk Band Alcohol Program
Heiltsuk Band Council
P.O. Box 880
Waglisla, B.C. V0T 1Z0
(604) 957-2381

Hey-Way'noqu' Healing Circle
Addictions Society
206 - 33 East Broadway Street
Vancouver, B.C. V5T 1V4
(604) 874-1831

Interior Indian Friendship Society
125 Palm Street
Kamloops, B.C. V2B 8J7
(604) 376-1296

Iskut First Nation NNADAP Program
Iskut Band Council
General Delivery
Iskut, B.C. V0J 1K0
(604) 234-3331

Kitkatla Drug & Alcohol Program
Kitkatla, B.C. V0V 1C0
(604) 638-9305

Kitselas Village Drug & Alcohol Program
4562 Queensway Drive
Terrace, B.C. V8G 3X6
(604) 635-5084

Kitsumkalum Drug & Alcohol Program
P.O. Box 544
Terrace, B.C. V8G 4B5
(604) 635-6177

Klahoose Drug & Alcohol Program
P.O. Box 9
Squirrel Cove, B.C. V0P 1K0
(604) 935-6650

L'ah Tsuten Alcohol & Drug Program
Necoslie Indian Band
P.O. Box 1329
Fort St. James, B.C. V0J 1P0
(604) 996-7171

Lake Babine Drug & Alcohol Program
Carrier Sekani tribal council
P.O. Box 879
Burns Lake, B.C. V0J 1E0
(604) 692-7555

Lax Kw'alaams Alcohol & Drug
Abuse Program
Lax Kw'alaams Band Council
P.O. Box 992
Port Simpson, B.C. V0V 1H0
(604) 565-2387

Lhahtsoneh Program
c/o Nechako Centre
2000-15th Avenue
Prince George, B.C. V2M 1S2
(604) 565-2387

Lil'wat Drug & Alcohol Abuse Program
Mount Currie Band Council
P.O. Box 165
Mount Currie, B.C. V0N 2K0
(604) 894-6115

Longhouse A.A.
2595 Franklin Street
Vancouver, B.C. V5K 1X5
(604) 254-4531

Lower Similkameen & Upper Similkameen
Drug & Alcohol Program
P.O. Box 100
Keremeos, B.C. V0X 1N0
(604) 499-5528

Lytton Alcohol Program
Lytton Indian Band
P.O. Box 20
Lytton, B.C. V0K 1Z0
(604) 455-2304

Masset Drug & Alcohol Program
P.O. Box 189
Masset, B.C. V0T 1M0
(604) 626-3337

McLeod Lake Drug & Alcohol Program
McLeod Lake, B.C. V0J 2G0
(604) 750-4415

Metlakatla Drug & Alcohol Program
P.O. Box 459
Prince Rupert, B.C. V8J 3R2

Musqueam Drug & Alcohol Program
6370 Salish Drive
Vancouver, B.C. V6N 2C6
(604) 263-3261

Nanaimo Drug & Alcohol Program
1145 Totem Road
Nanaimo, B.C. V9R 1H1
(604) 753-3481

Native Alcohol & Drug Counselling Service
Cowichan Band Council
203-262 Station Street
Duncan, B.C. V9L 1N1
(604) 748-1141

Native Alcohol Counsellor
4770 Johnson
Port Alberni, B.C. V9Y 5M3
(604) 723-6292

Nautley Drug & Alcohol Counselling
Fraser Lake Band
P.O. Box 36
Fort Fraser, B.C. V0J 1N0
(604) 690-7409

Nazko Drug & Alcohol Program
P.O. Box 4534
Quesnel, B.C. V2J 3Y9
(604) 992-9810

Nimpkish Yuyatsi Alcohol
Counselling Program
P.O. Box 290
Alert Bay, B.C. V0N 1A0
(604) 974-5522

Nlaka'pamux Nation Tribal Council
P.O. Box 430
Lytton, B.C. V0K 1Z0
(604) 455-2711

North Thompson Drug & Alcohol Program
P.O. Box 220
Barriere, B.C. V0E 1E0
(604) 672-9995

Numawta Counsellor Program
Box 65
Bella Coola, B.C. V0T 1C0
(604) 799-5525

Osoyoos Drug & Alcohol Program
R.R. #3, Site 25, Comp. 1
Oliver, B.C. V0H 1T0
(604) 498-4906

Outreach Program
144 George Street
Prince George, B.C. V2L 1P9
(604) 564-2444

Pavillion Drug & Alcohol Program
P.O. Box 609
Cache Creek, B.C. V0K 1H0
(604) 256-4202

Penelakut Drug & Alcohol Program
P.O. Box 360
Chemainus, B.C. V0R 1K0
(604) 246-2321

Penticton Drug & Alcohol Program
R.R. #2, Site 80, Comp. 19
Penticton, B.C. V2A 6J7
(604) 493-0048

Quatsino NNADAP Program
Quatsino First Nations Office
P.O. Box 100
Coal Harbour, B.C. V0N 1K0
(604) 949-6245

Round Lake Treatment Centre
R.R. #3, Comp. 10
Grandview Flats North
Armstrong, B.C. V0E 1B0
(604) 546-3077
Fax: 546-3227

Saanich Tribal Drug & Alcohol Program
Tseycum Band Council
P.O. Box 2595
Sidney, B.C. V8L 4C1
(604)656-0858

Saulteau Drug & Alcohol Program
Carrier Sekani Tribal Council
Box 414
Chetwynd, B.C. V0X 1J0
(604) 788-3955

Seabird Island and Scowlitz First Nations
Anti-Drug Program
Seabird Island Band Administration
Box 650
Agissaz, B.C. V0M 1A0
(604) 796-2177

Seton Lake Drug & Alcohol Program
Shalath, B.C. V0N 3C0
(604) 259-8227

Sechelt Indian Band Alternative Program
Sechelt Indian Band
P.O. Box 740
Sechelt, B.C. V0N 3A0
(604) 688-3017

Sliammon Drug & Alcohol Program
R.R. #2, Sliammon Road
Powell River, B.C. V8A 4Z3
(604) 483-2166

Soda Creek NNADAP Project
Soda Creek Band Office
Site 15, Comp. 2, R.R. #4
Williams Lake, B.C. V2G 4M8
(604) 297-6323

Squamish Indian Band Alcohol
& Drug Program
Box 86131
North Vancouver, B.C. V7L 4J5
(604) 985-7711

Stellaquo Drug & Alcohol Program
Carrier Sekani Tribal Council
P.O. Box 760
Fraser Lake, B.C. V0J 1S0
(604) 699-8741

Stewart Trembleaur Alcohol Project
Stewart Trembleaur Band
P.O. Box 670
Fort St. James, B.C. V0J 1S0
(604) 648-3213

Sto:lo Tribal Council NNADAP
P.O. Box 310
Sardis, B.C. V2R 1A7
(604) 858-3366

Stoney Creek Drug & Alcohol Program
Carrier Sekani Tribal Council
P.O. Box 1069
Vanderhoof, B.C. V0J 3A0
(604) 567-9293

Sugar Cane Alcohol Program
Williams Lake Indian Band
R.R. #3, Sugar Cane, Box 4
Williams Lake, B.C. V2G 1M3
(604) 296-3507

SUNS (Sober Urban Native Society)
3555 Fourth Avenue
P.O. Box 1164
Port Alberni, B.C. V9Y 7M1
(604) 724-9666

Taaxwi Laas Native Alcohol Abuse Program
Skidegate Band Council
P.O. Box 699
Queen Charlotte, B.C. V0T 1S0
(604) 599-4496

Tahltan Band Council Substance Abuse
Telegraph Creek, B.C. V0J 2W0
(604) 235-3241

Tahltan Tribal Council NNADAP
Dease Lake, B.C. V0C 1L0
(604) 771-5151

Takla Lake NNADAP
Takla Landing via
Fort St. James, B.C. V0J 2T0
Takla Landing 1-L Radio 0711

Taku River Tlingits NNADAP
P.O. Box 132
Atlin, B.C. V0W 1A0
(604) 651-7776

Tansi Family Violence Program
P.O. Box 418
Chetwynd, B.C. V0C 1J0
(604) 788-2969

Tillicum Haus Native Friendship Centre
927 Haliburton Street
Nanaimo, B.C. V9R 5K1
(604) 753-8291

Tl'azt'en Nations Drug & Alcohol Program
Carrier Sekani Tribal Council
Box 670
Fort St. James, B.C. V0J 1P0
(604) 648-3212

Tsawout Drug & Alcohol Program
P.O. Box 121
Saanichton, B.C. V0S 1M0
(604) 652-9101

Ulkatcho Council Drug & Alcohol Program
Anahim Lake, B.C. V0L 1C0
(604) 742-3260

Treatment Centres

Haisla Support and Recovery Centre
P.O. Box 1036
Kitamaat, B.C. V0T 2B0
(604) 632-7644
Fax: 632-5719

Hey'way'noqu' Healing Circle for Addictions
206-33 East Broadway
Vancouver, B.C. V5T 1V4
(604) 874-1831
Fax: 874-5235

Kakawis Family Development Centre
Box 17
Tofino, B.C. V0R 2Z0
(604) 725-3951
Fax: 725-4285

Ktunaxa-Kinbasket Wellness Centre
Box 17, R.R. #1, Site 7
Highway 2
Creston, B.C. V0B 1G0
(604) 428-5516
Fax: 428-5235

Nenqayni Treatment Centre
P.O. Box 2528
Williams Lake, B.C. V2G 4P2
(604) 989-0301
Fax: 989-0307

Northern Native Family Services
1274 Fifth Avenue
Prince George, B.C. V2L 3L2
(604) 562-3591

Sicamous Lodge Spallumcheen
Recovery Home
Spallumcheen Indian Band
P.O. Box 430
Enderby, B.C. V0E 1V0
(604) 838-9565
Fax: 838-2131

Three Sisters Haven
General Delivery
Telegraph Creek, B.C. V0J 2W0
(604)235-3120
Fax: 235-3118

Tsow-Tun Le Lum Society
Substance Abuse Treatment Centre
Box 370
Lantzville, B.C. V0R 2H0
(604) 390-3123
FaxL 390-3119

Wilp Si'satxw Community Healing Centre
Box 249
Kitwanga, B.C. V0J 2A0
(604) 849-5211
Fax: 849-5374